MW00479912

CONFESSIONS
of a
KLUTZ
CONFESSIONS SERIES #1

A ROMANTIC COMEDY BY

ABIGAIL DAVIES

Confessions Of A Klutz
Second Edition.
Copyright © 2018 Abigail Davies.
All rights reserved.
Published: Abigail Davies 2018

No parts of this book may be reproduced in any form without written consent from the author. Except in the use of brief quotations in a book review.

This book is a piece of fiction. Any names, characters, businesses, places or events are a product of the author's imagination or are used fictitiously. Any resemblance to persons living or dead, events or locations is purely coincidental.

This book is licensed for your personal enjoyment only. This book may not be resold or given away to other people. If you are reading this book and have not purchased it for your use only, then you should return it to your favorite book retailer and purchase your own copy. Thank you for respecting the author's work.

Editing:
Josie Cruize
Jennifer Roberts-Hall
Proofreading:
Judy's Proofreading
Cover Design:
Abigail Davies at Pink Elephant Designs
Formatting:
Abigail Davies at Pink Elephant Designs

Acknowledgments

Where do I even start? *cracks knuckles and takes a deep breath*

This book wasn't planned at all, but it has been one of my favorite to write. Writing this book truly helped me to escape and I loved every second of it. Allowing the funny me to come out has been refreshing and I will most definitely be writing more books like this!

I have lots of people to thank but I'll try to keep it as short as possible.

First and most important thanks go to my two girls. They inspire me every single day and I'm sure I annoy them to no end. A special thank you to my eldest daughter for helping me name a "character" in this book.

As always, thank you to my hubby, Mike. He's awesome and puts up with me so is doing his good deed in life!

Thank you to my bestie, Danielle. As always, you're there to bounce ideas off, to laugh with me, and let me moan at you. Vife for life! *peace sign*

Thank you to my beta readers: Amanda, Angela, Liza, Paige, and Yvonne! All of your feedback always makes my stories so much better!

To my editors Josie and Jennifer. Thank you so much for your input on rewriting this story. I appreciate it so much!

To my proofreader, Judy, thank you so much! She's always there to explain things to me, even when we can't work out what the button inside a handset is! (It's a plunger by the way…*weird*.)

A huge thank you to Linda! Having you on my team now completely de-stresses me. Thank you to you and your whole team. I'm so glad I found you!

Thank you to the awesome ladies in my reader group, "Abi's Aces." You provided me with TONS of stories to use in the headers in this book and I can't tell you how much it means for every one of you wanting to be a part of this book!

A huge thank you to all the bloggers, readers, and authors that share all of my book posts. Being part of this community is awesome and I now have friends all around the world.

Last but by no means least: thank you to all my amazing readers, for all of the messages I receive on a daily basis. It warms my heart so much to know that you enjoy my stories. I hope you love this one as much as I do!

Thank you for allowing me to do what I love most and tell these stories! <3

Confession One: I was a klutz.
I thought I'd grow out of it, but evidently I didn't.
It's not fun to look like a fumbling toddler when you're
twenty-six.

Confession Two: I had a standing appointment at the
local ER.
It wasn't by choice that I knew all the doctors names—it
was necessity.
But that was about to change.

Confession Three: I hated the sun yet I lived in LA where
it always shone.
I supposed that was one plus to being sent to New York
for the next eight weeks.

That was until I got there.

Arm veins, dimples, and THE sexiest voice known to
man were my weakness,

and he had every single one of them.

Confession Four: He was my new boss.
I could control myself though, right?

The city of dreams…a klutz's worst nightmare.
Eight weeks. A klutz. And a drool worthy boss.
What did you get when you crossed a klutz with a GQ
model lookalike?
I was about to find out.

Note from the author

This book is DEFINITELY based on true events.

I'm a klutz and proud!

For my youngest daughter, Faith.
I'm sorry I passed you the klutz gene. I'll forever be there to
catch you when you fall...over nothing.

Chapter 1
CONFESSION #35: I ONCE TRIPPED OVER
A WIRELESS PHONE.

I trudged my way down the hallway lined with offices on either side. All the doors were open, and I could see each person sitting at their desks, silently getting on with their work. This floor was so different from the one back home in LA. You couldn't think for the amount of noise everyone made, which was why I always had my earphones in, listening to whichever latest show had taken my fancy. Right now I was in an epic *Game Of Thrones* binge marathon. That was until my supervisor, Elliot, had marched me to the CFO's office.

My lip curled as I thought about Della, the CFO, sending me to New York for the next eight weeks. I was one of six assistants in the LA office, and I was the only one without a family, so it was me who they chose to come to New York to fill in for someone who had been in a car wreck. I had no idea why they sent me though because I did the bare minimum and even that was a stretch for me at times.

I enjoyed working for Taylor Industries more than the other twenty-three jobs I'd had since graduating from college four years ago. Yes, I'd been keeping count, and no, it wasn't because I was bad at them. I just got bored. My attention span was the same as a fish.

This latest job was the best I'd had so far, and the last two months had been awesome. My workload was emailed to me each morning, and once I was done with it, I could get on with my binging.

I knew a little of what Taylor Industries did, but nothing major. After all, I basically just wrote the meeting notes up and did general admin work. But I knew they bought other businesses and either stripped them down and sold them, or turned them around and kept the corporations under their belt.

The latest one they had gathered was to be stripped down, but I knew if they kept it, they could make a very lucrative profit. Not that I planned to tell Della that. I wouldn't be listened to, anyway.

But now I was here, in New York, about to become Mr. Taylor's PA. I hadn't met Mr. Taylor, as he rarely came into the LA office. Normally, in an office there would be gossip about the boss—I knew this on account of the many jobs I'd had. But there was zero about this boss. He was a complete mystery to everyone.

I came to a stop outside of Mr. Taylor's office. A sleek, white desk sat in front of it and off to the side a little. I swallowed and ran my tongue over the split in my lip. It was just my luck that the day before I met the boss who owned the whole company that I would fall and not only snap the heel off one of my shoes but also smack my face off the granite floor.

I shook my head to expel my thoughts and walked toward the desk. I placed my coat over the back and my bag on the seat. There was no doubt this would be my workplace while I was here. There was definitely no way I'd be able to slack off, on account of him being able to see my computer through the glass windows separating his office from the hallway.

Steeling myself and straightening my back, I took a deep breath, ready to go and meet my new boss—or old one…whatever. I spun around just as a booming voice called out, "You're late, Miss Scott. Get in my office."

I searched for the voice and where it came from, and then I spotted a speaker attached to the phone on the desk. I trailed my hands down my white blouse, smoothing it out along with my gray pencil skirt and stepped toward his door. I knocked and waited for a beat, but when there was no command to come in, I opened it up.

A hunched figure sat behind the sleek desk that was much the same as the one outside, only this one was twice the size. I cleared my throat. "Good morning, Mr. Taylor. I'm sorry I was a few minutes late. I wasn't given the code—"

"First rule," his deep voice interrupted.

I widened my eyes at the baritone of it, hating how the smoothness caused goose bumps to spread along my skin and a flutter to explode in my *downstairs region*.

"Don't blame anything or anybody for being late. Own your mistakes."

"But—"

"Second rule," he grated out. "Don't interrupt me."

"Like you just did?" I whispered, but not loud enough for him to hear me.

"What was that?"

"Nothing," I chirped. *Why had he still not looked up at me?*

"Third and final rule." He paused. "Close the door when you come into my office."

"Oh! Of course." I scrambled behind me and shut the door without taking my eyes off his bent head. I was only able to make out his dark-blond hair, longer on the top and flopping forward but shorter on the sides.

His head flicked up at the sound of the door clicking shut, and the breath left my body in a rush. His dark-blue gaze ran up my body, stopping at my eyes, assessing me in a calculating way. My cheeks heated at his attention.

A smattering of hair covered his jaw, his cheekbones so sharp they could cut glass. And those lashes—it was so unfair that men were blessed with the long, thick ones. Hot damn, he even had a chin dimple. What was it about dimples that immediately made a woman turn to mush?

I was preoccupied with taking him in, noting his charcoal suit jacket hanging on the back of his chair, his white dress shirt rolled up to the elbows and showing arm veins. Oh, God, I was a sucker for arm veins. They were so…*manly*.

My gaze finally rolled up over his dark-blue tie before stopping on his lips that were…spread into a grim line. *Shit. How long had I been staring?*

"If you've quite finished, Miss Scott, we have a schedule to go over."

"I—" I cleared my throat. "Of course, Mr. Taylor. Let me grab my tablet to—"

He huffed impatiently, pushed a piece of paper across his desk, and placed his pen on top of it, silently telling me to use it. Right. I could do this. I could totally sit opposite this juicy beef burger of a man and write down what he told me without disappearing into Vi Dreamland, where all the men were as sexy and as cut as this one, and fanning me as I sat on my chaise lounge.

Dammit, I was going there again.

I shook my arms out. He watched me and lifted his brows, but I ignored it, ready to get to work. Eight weeks. Forty work days—possibly a few more if he was a tyrant. I bet he was a tyrant in the bedroom.

Stop it!

"Right, yes." I pulled away from the door. "Let's do thi—"

No. *No, no, no.* The sound of ripping material echoed around the room like the bass of a guitar in a crowded arena. I slammed my eyes shut, praying—hoping like hell—that what happened wasn't...

Yep. Yep, it was. I felt the air flowing up my thigh, and when I looked down, the seam to my skirt was ripped all the way up to my hip. I slapped my hand over it, concealing the white cotton granny panties I had decided to wear today. Dammit. Why couldn't I have at least chosen some sexy lace ones?

Great first impression, Vi. Just...*great.*

———

I stood, pulled my coat off the back of my chair and pushed my arms through the sleeves. Thank God it covered the disaster that was my skirt.

I'd managed to pin it together with five safety pins, but all it'd done was make me look like a goth kid—the ones who walked around with their hair in their face, and their eyes rimmed with black kohl eyeliner. I never understood kids like that. Why did they paint one fingernail black? What did it mean? And don't even get me started on those jeans that may as well be painted on them, much like the nail polish. I wondered what they'd look like if they laughed? Or was that against their religion or something?

Tilting my head to the side, I stared at the safety pins. I could totally pull off the goth look if I put my mind to it. Not the jeans though—I didn't want to wrestle with my clothes.

I winced as my new heels cut into the back of my feet. I'd had to keep them on *all day*. It was a crime to have to keep your feet enclosed in them, but I had no choice because Mr. CEO had the air conditioner on outside his office. It was winter. In New York, for Pete's sake!

Shaking my head, I picked the tablet up to finish off the last of organizing his schedule back at the hotel, but I paused when he walked out of his office. I flicked my gaze over to him, but he wasn't looking my way. Instead, he was frowning down at his cell—a frown that I itched to smooth out with my fingers. Was his tan skin as soft as it looked?

I finally pulled my greedy eyes away from my hunk of a boss and slipped the tablet into my bag.

"Miss Scott."

Holy shit. It should be illegal to have a voice like that.

"Yes, Mr. Taylor?"

He stepped closer. His cologne wrapped around me like a warm blanket on a winter night. I took an extra deep breath of the musk and earthy scent that was like crack to an addict. His dark-blue eyes bore into me. "I have a last-minute meeting, and I need you to take notes."

Goddammit all to hell! It was 6:00 p.m. I'd been here for eleven hours, and all I could imagine was the giant jacuzzi tub in my suite, begging me to sit my ass in it and not move until I resembled a dried-up prune. *Isn't a prune already a dried fruit?* Hmm, I'll ask Google when I got back to the hotel.

"I—" I shuffled on my feet, wincing again as my heels pinched my skin.

He looked back down at his cell as he said, "It's on the east side. Let's go." He spun around and headed toward the elevators.

I grabbed my bag and hobbled after him, gaining me some weird looks from the other people—mainly men— walking around on this floor. The women stared at me knowingly, offering me pitiful smiles. It was like we were all in a club where we all knew what the pain of wearing brand-new heels was like, but we had to endure it for…wait, *why was I enduring it?*

The elevator doors opened as soon as Mr. Taylor stopped in front of them, almost as if they knew he was coming—or maybe he had a superpower? Now that would be cool. Oh my God, was I working for a super-hero? Actually, he kind of looked more like a villain. Hmm… I wondered what his costume was?

We both stepped inside, and the doors closed behind us, leaving only me and Mr. Villain in the metal box that could plunge us to our deaths if it was so inclined. *Shit, don't think like that, Vi.*

Jesus H. Christ, I was driving myself insane with all my rambling thoughts.

Neither of us talked as the elevator took us down to the main floor. The doors whooshed open, and we both stepped out. Wetness trickled on the back of my ankle, so I stopped, leaning my hand against the wall to see what the sensation was.

"Son of a batch of cookies!"

Why? Why, oh, why did I wear brand-new heels for my first day of work? They'd shredded my feet, and now all I wanted to do was hold my feet to my chest and rock them back and forth, telling them it'll get better. Yet, I knew I was lying because these were the only pair of heels I'd brought with me. Someone should tell those gangsters that ran around the streets that they don't need to be pulling fingernails off people's hands. Instead, they should make people wear a brand-new pair of heels as a form of torture.

I yanked the offending things off my feet, closed my eyes, and moaned as the cold floor seeped through my skin. Now *that* was heaven.

"What the hell are you doing?"

I squeaked at the growling voice that vibrated down my ear, and when I turned my head, Mr. Taylor was standing a couple of inches away from me, his chest nearly touching my arm.

"I'm removing the torture devices."

He frowned at me, an impatient look on his face.

I held them up between us and explained, "They've cut my feet open and—"

"Fuck me, why the hell would Della do this?"

I opened my mouth, about to ask what he was talking about when he continued.

"No, I know why." He ran a hand down his face. "She's trying to get her own back for me sleeping with her senior year." His fingers curled around my bicep as he pulled me along with him toward the doors. "More than a decade later, and she's still trying to get revenge for the one-night stand."

My eyes widened as he talked, his tone deep and threatening. Who the hell shit in his Cocoa Puffs?

He pushed me through the turnstile door and headed for a black, idling car at the edge of the sidewalk. He pulled open the door and waved his hand at me to get in. I did as he silently said, shuffling over on the seat.

He slipped inside and slammed the door behind him. "Reels and Dew, Jeeves. I need to be there in ten minutes, so step on it."

I rolled my lips and tried my hardest to keep in the chuckle that was desperate to break free at the sound of his name. After I was sure I wouldn't laugh, I leaned to the right and spotted the driver who had picked me up at the airport.

"Hey, Jeeves!"

"Miss Scott." He nodded, a smirk lifting the corners of his mouth.

Mr. Taylor grumbled, and I turned to face him. His thumbs paused over the screen of his cell, and he turned, his gaze meeting mine. "Can you back up?"

My eyes widened as I realized how close to him I was. I shuffled away from him, my thigh flush with the door as silence reigned around us. *I hated silence.* Clutching the other side of my skirt, I stared out the window while Jeeves weaved in and out of traffic. He finally stopped in front of another metal and glass building seven minutes later.

Mr. Taylor pushed out of the car, his gaze still connected with his cell. I gripped onto my heels as I shuffled over the seat, exited, and walked beside him into the building. I blanched when we stepped inside yet another elevator, and I realized I was going to have to put the death traps back on.

"Cock suckers," I murmured as I bent my knees so I could slip them back on.

"Excuse me?"

I rolled my eyes, fed up that today wasn't over yet. I hadn't even managed to watch a minute of anything because I'd been so busy trying to figure out the system he used. These eight weeks were going to kill me.

I waved the shoe in the air between us, nearly hitting him in the face as I straightened up. "Do you know what it's like to have to wear these things?"

He opened his mouth, but I didn't let him talk.

"Torture, pure torture. And now I have to put them back on while my foot is bleeding." I gritted my teeth as I stared at his wide eyes. "I'm going to be leaving a trail of—What are you doing?"

I yanked my foot out of his grasp and stumbled away from his crouched position.

"I'm checking your foot. I didn't realize you were bleeding."

"Well, you wouldn't because you went all grrr and pulled me out of the office and—"

"Grrr?" He raised his brow, a grin shadowing his face.

I parted my lips as I stared at his face, my mouth salivating at the sight of him. Jesus, he was even more sexy with those lips spread wide. They were so full, and they'd look like perfection if they were between my legs.

Shit, I went there again.

He wrapped his hand around my ankle, my skin tingled at his touch. I shook my head and swallowed. "Yeah, you know, all caveman—You spunktrumpet!"

"Keep still," he commanded, his deep voice echoing around us as he assessed my foot. He gazed up at me. "Should be okay once it's cleaned." His hand moved upward, and I didn't think he even realized he was doing it.

His smooth palm grazed the back of my knee. My pulse quickened, and my breaths sawed in and out of my body. I was practically panting like a sex addict in a whorehouse. A shiver rolled down my spine, and I sunk my teeth into my bottom lip. He zoned in on the action, his eyes growing darker as his hand tightened on my soft skin.

The door opened, a ping echoed, and it was like a bucket of ice-cold water was being thrown over him. He pulled away, yanked his hand back, and stood, clearing his throat. "Leave the heels off," he muttered. "We won't be long. I'll give you a ride back to the hotel when we're done."

You could give me a ride anytime.

Chapter 2

CONFESSION #78: I FELL OVER AND SCRAPED MY KNEES...WHILE I WAS CARRYING A BABY.

I stumbled out of my hotel room and toward the elevator, my eyes small slits as I tried to wake myself up. It wasn't that I was tired, per se. I just freaking hated mornings. Who the hell decided everyone would have to wake up at an ungodly hour to start work? Why couldn't we all wake up at say, noon, then stroll into our offices leisurely and do our allotted hours before coming home?

All I was saying was that Dolly was wrong. I wasn't working nine to five—it was six thirty right now, and the sun wasn't even fully up as I walked toward the main reception area. The guy who helped me with my bags when I'd arrived a couple of days ago was standing next to the main door, his eyes focused and fresh-faced. *Ugh, morning people were the worst.*

"Good morning," he chirped, just like the birds I was sure were singing outside.

"Hey." I staggered to a stop in front of him, my lips spread into a stern line. "I have two very important questions for you, Al."

"Sure, go ahead." He grinned, his face full of hope that he could help.

I held up a finger. "First, I need coffee—a huge jug of the stuff. Where's the best place?"

His lips spread into a wider grin as he said, "Wait here, Miss Scott."

He wandered off. Well, wander was a relative term. He jogged toward the bar that sat behind two ornate glass doors to the left. A couple of minutes later he returned with a thermos in his hand.

"I didn't know if you liked cream and sugar, but I added them—"

"Oh, God, Al." I practically tackled him when he got within a few feet of me. I ripped it out of his hand and unscrewed the lid. "You're my new favorite doorman," I said and took a huge gulp. I tilted my head to the side. "Although I thought you were a bellboy?"

He chuckled, but a blush started to cover his sculpted cheekbones. His blue eyes skirted away from mine as he moved back to the post he was standing at a few minutes ago. He cleared his throat, standing at his full height—which, by my awesome estimation, was about six feet. Give or take five inches. "I'm kind of both." He shrugged. "There was a second thing, Miss Scott…"

I took another couple of sips, moaned as the coffee flowed over my taste buds, and pulled it away from my mouth. "Ah, yes. I need a taxi to take me to…" I trailed off, not remembering the address of the new office. *Shit-pouches.* I'd been here for two days, so it wasn't as if I should have memorized it, right?

Screwing the lid back on the thermos, I then placed it on the floor between my feet, pulled out the tablet I was given to handle all of Mr. Taylor's schedule, and logged into it. I searched for the address and reeled it off to Al. He nodded, looking out of the glass doors where the sun was just starting to come out—barely. Stupid early morning meetings. Who the hell decided having one at 7:00 a.m. was a good idea?

"Mr. Taylor left right before you stepped off the elevator and—"

"Wait, what?" He was here, but he didn't even offer me a ride? How *rude!* "He was here?"

"Uh-huh." Al's brows drew down in confusion. "He owns the hotel, so he lives on the top floor."

"Of course he does," I practically sneered. My gaze roved around the empty foyer and landed on the grandfather clock standing proudly next to the reception desk. "Shit, I have fifteen minutes to get there." I bent down and picked up my liquid gold before rushing out the doors with Al on my tail.

What the actual! *Cold...too cold.* How the hell did people live in this arctic weather? My nips could cut glass!

Al hailed a cab, and when one darted toward us and came to a stop, he told him the address and opened the back door for me. I practically jumped into it, pulling my coat tighter around me—my *way too thin for New York* coat.

"Should get you there in ten minutes, miss," the middle-aged man with graying hair at his temples said as he clicked a few buttons on his dash and darted out into oncoming traffic.

My shoulder banged into the door, and my thermos rolled off my lap and onto the floor. The driver didn't look fazed in the slightest as I gripped the door handle.

Is that what these were here for? To hold onto so you didn't die?

He rushed through the streets, taking turns left, right, and center—literally—and pulled up alongside an office building. They all seemed to look the same in cities. All this modern-day steel and glass gave me a giant headache and vertigo. Why couldn't people understand it wasn't sexy to stand on the fiftieth floor gazing out of the window at the skyline? What if the glass pane suddenly broke free as you were leaning against it? Then all you were was a splat on the asphalt before street cleaners swept you away and the glass was replaced.

I shivered, both from the cold and my mind's image as I stepped out of the cab and handed the driver some bills. I ran as fast as I could, wincing as the new heels started to bite into the sides of my feet, but I ignored it as I jabbed my finger on the button of the elevator. The doors slid open, and I practically jumped inside and pressed the button for the floor I needed to be on.

As soon as I stepped out of the elevator, I frowned at the lack of activity. Half the lights weren't on, and there was zero noise. I moved toward my desk and Mr. Taylor's office and noticed him sitting in his chair with his eyes closed. *Shouldn't he already be in the meeting room?*

"Mr. Taylor?" I ventured, my voice low.

His eyes sprang open, his dark-blue orbs wild until they settled on me.

I shuffled. "Wasn't there meant to be a meeting?"

He grunted and stood, swiping his jacket off the back of his chair. "Yes. But they canceled."

"Canceled?" I asked, swallowing as he stepped toward me.

"It's business, Miss Scott. Meetings get canceled all the time."

"Right." I cleared my throat and gripped the thermos tighter. "But wasn't that an important meeting regarding the company you wanted to buy?"

A muscle in his jaw danced as he clenched his jaw. I could practically feel the anger vibrating off him.

"It was." He swiped his hand through his hair and gripped it as he looked up at the ceiling. "Shit. Fuck." He started to pace the small space in front of his desk. "I needed this deal to go through. It would have put us on the map this side of the States."

"You did say it happened all the ti—"

"I know," he interrupted, his tone sharp. "But not to me."

I raised a brow, a comment on the end of my tongue. Did he think he was invincible?

"I've worked too hard to just let everything slip away. I *needed* that meeting."

I glanced down at his chest that was heaving on each breath he took and looked back into his eyes. I could see how passionate he was about his company, and I related to that passion. There was only one thing I felt like that about, but I didn't think I could cope if it was taken away from me.

"Let me see what I can do," I said and stepped back.

"What can you do?" he asked, a frown on his face.

I shrugged. "Maybe I can talk my way into another meeting. You never know."

"I—"

I swiped my hand through the air. "I got this." I didn't know what he was going to say, but it sounded like the right thing to reply to him.

Now I just had to work out what I could do to persuade them to give us another meeting.

———

I bit down on the lid of my pen, my gaze zoned in on Mr. Taylor as he stood from his chair at the head of the table. He demanded everyone's attention during the head of departments meeting as he undid his cuff links, pocketed them, and rolled his sleeves up. I couldn't stop staring at his movements. I was like an old man—one who hadn't gotten his dick wet in years—watching a stripper.

I could confirm that I one hundred percent had a lady boner.

He studied each person at the table, then his gaze stopped on me. His straight face and guarded eyes gave nothing away, but yet I still squirmed in my seat. *Jeez, Louise, I needed to calm myself down.*

Today was day six, and there hadn't been a word said between us since I said I'd get us another meeting from the people who had canceled. I was working my ass off to try and butter up the main person—Mr. Johnson—and that included his PA too.

I didn't mind that Mr. Taylor hadn't spoken to me, though, because sometimes people were awesome to look at but douchebags to talk to. Maybe he was one of *those* kinds of guys?

I needed at least forty-eight hours to confirm or deny that.

For sure, I thought there'd be gossip about him, allowing me to determine it sooner rather than later, but there'd been nothing. Zero. Zilch. Nada. Maybe he dazzled everyone with his strong jaw and dimpled chin, and they were put under some kind of spell, causing them not to utter a bad word about him?

Oh! Maybe he had the kind of skills all the hip vampires and werewolves had these days. Talking about vampires, was anyone else brokenhearted over the fact that Damon and Stefan wouldn't be on our screens anymore?

"Scott."

My gaze clashed with Mr. Taylor's, and I opened my mouth, about to ask him to repeat himself, but he continued on.

"She'll be filling in for Sheila until Christmas. Jayla?" His attention was on the woman sitting three seats down on his right. "Do you have applications for the position yet?"

"Yes, Mr. Taylor." She batted her eyelashes, and I raised a brow, wondering if she'd take flight like a butterfly. Someone should tell her she was as obvious as a flashing red sign advertising an adult store. *"Get your dildos here!"*

"Good, I want the position filled as soon as possible." He moved his gaze to mine, something flashing in the depths of his eyes, causing me to scrunch my nose. He zoned in on the action, his hand clenching into a fist at his side.

I glanced away, not able to keep the contact going for long. He was just too…intense.

He continued on, walking toward the wall of windows as he talked about the latest ventures in business. I got lost after the third sentence and flipped to an open page on my notebook. My pen moved at lightning speed as my mind ran away with me.

There were many kinds of artists out there, all using different forms and tools. Me? I liked to use ballpoint pens. I may not have been able to use oil paints or watercolors, but I could draw the shit out of people. Realistic was something I loved to do, but my absolute passion was to draw caricatures. Not too out there, though. I still wanted people to recognize who they were. I supposed you'd call what I do comic strips. I called them my fun moments. Did anyone else laugh at themselves all the time? Because I did, and I'd say I was freaking hilarious.

I stopped and tilted my head to the side. The pad of my finger grazed over the head of Mr. Taylor—the one I drew, not the real one. He was standing twice the size as the rest of the people around the table, all of them with speech bubbles coming from their mouths. I snorted at what I'd written above Jayla: Would you like a blow—

A hand landed on my notepad, and I squeaked. Tips of fingers grazed over my knuckles, and my breath stalled when a forearm came into view. *Shit. I'd recognize that forearm anywhere.*

Looking around, I spotted a guy toward the end of the table talking, everyone's attention on him. I turned my head to face Mr. Taylor's. He raised a brow, his blue-eyed gaze flicking from me to the paper.

I swallowed and opened my mouth, about to say… what? I didn't freaking know! But he was staring right at his caricature face, which was depicted as staring out of the window.

He bent down, moving into my space and whispered what the thought bubble above it said. "I'll use my cheekbones to cut through this glass and escape these kiss asses."

He shook his head at me, a small movement, and

pulled his warm hold off mine, his pointer finger dragging over the top of my hand. I shivered, and goose bumps trailed over my skin. Jesus, I'd read about that in those sappy romance books, but I never thought it would actually happen. Was I in an alternate universe?

He stepped away, allowing me to take a breath that I hadn't known I was holding. I slammed my book closed and paid attention as the guy continued to talk. I couldn't stop my gaze from skirting over to Mr. Taylor as he sauntered toward the head of the table. I stuttered a breath when I found his eyes fixated on me. I couldn't look away, the dark-blue orbs catching me in their web. *Why the hell couldn't I look away?*

"So, I think it would be very lucrative," the unnamed guy said.

Mr. Taylor snapped his attention to the guy, opening his mouth but closing it again when his cell went off. He flicked his gaze back to me briefly, only there wasn't an ounce of what was there mere seconds ago. Did I imagine the whole thing?

Of course you imagined it! He wouldn't be staring at your lips like they were a piece of medium-rare steak—best way to cook it by the way. I didn't want my steak to be a piece of rubber, thank you very much.

Mr. Taylor huffed out a breath as he pulled his cell out of his pocket. "I have to take this. We'll talk more after I've had the meeting with the potential new venture on Friday."

I grinned. I'd managed to not only work my magic to get the meeting back on, but I'd also been doing my research, and I was dying to show Mr. Taylor my plans.

He clicked on his cell screen, moving toward the back of the room as everyone filed out like bats out of hell.

Jayla sneered at me as she walked by, and I raised my brow in return. What the hell was butterfly's problem?

By the time the stampede halted, there was only me and Mr. Taylor left in the room. I swallowed, stood, and smoothed down the light-blue blouse tucked into my skinny, ankle-grazer pants. When I checked out my ass in the mirror this morning, it could only be described as awesome, but it was the kind of awesome where if you sat too fast, you could rip them—kind of like with my skirt last week, the one that was now stuffed into my suitcase waiting for me to try to fix it. *Try* being the optimum word. Sewing and I didn't go together, but it wasn't like I could afford to throw it out and replace it.

"Miss Scott?" he asked in a soft, raspy voice.

"Yes?" I shivered at Mr. Taylor saying my name like that but kept my attention focused on him, fascinated as he rolled down his sleeves methodically, his thumb and finger grasping his cuff link as he attached it to the cuff of his shirt.

"I'd really appreciate if you paid attention in my meetings." He moved on to the next sleeve and strode forward. "It is your job after all."

"I…" I swallowed against my dry throat and shifted backward.

He tilted his head, stopping a foot in front of me. Holding my breath, I flicked my gaze up at him, noting how tall he was. Jeez, why was everyone huge in New York? Or was that just because of my own height? Being a tiny human sucked sometimes.

He held his hand out to me, and I frowned down at it. What did he—

"The tablet, Miss Scott."

"Oh! Right, yes." I scrambled to pass it over to him,

hitting him in the stomach in the process. He grunted, his eyes closing briefly. Shit. I had just assaulted my new boss! I hadn't been here a full week, and I was already in deep doo-doo.

"I'm sor—"

"Don't." He straightened and swiped on the screen, his nostrils flaring as his breathing deepened. He was so close that if I were to reach out, I'd be touching—

"I see you've not been taking notes."

"I have, they're not on there." I lifted my notepad, waving it in the air like a flag. "They're on—hey!"

He grabbed the edge of the notepad, but I wasn't going to let go. I pulled on it, and he counteracted by yanking it. I stumbled but still didn't let go.

"It's…private," I told him.

He raised a brow as his other hand wrapped around my wrist. The pads of his warm fingers caressed the skin as he skimmed down my hand and relieved my grip on the notepad, one finger at a time.

"Please…" I murmured.

He dipped his head and flipped it open. His dark gaze scanned over the notes I'd written in shorthand during the meeting. He paused and turned the page.

"What's this?" he asked, his voice deeper.

I lifted up onto my tiptoes and focused on the airplane I had sketched while waiting in LAX airport. "Nothing." I lunged for it, but he held it out of reach and flipped the page. He stopped on the Harley I drew on Saturday, along with Jon Snow sitting on top of the beast. I grinned at the image because he looked total badass.

"Hmmm, doesn't seem like nothing."

I grabbed for it again, only this time I managed to

grip the edge and pull it out of his grasp. "Like I said, they're private, Mr. Taylor. I don't come into your...your hotel and ask to see your...erm..." I bit my bottom lip. "Your..."

"My?"

"Your...ugh." I spun around and stalked out of the room, whispering, "You can be such an as—"

"Remember I'm your boss, Miss Scott."

Fuckstickles, he heard me. I turned around, about to apologize, but the slight quirk of his lips caught me off guard.

"You may return to your desk." His brow lifted as if he was waiting for me to say something to him but I was completely lost and totally frazzled that he'd seen something I'd never let anybody but Ella, my cousin, look at. My drawings were mine, and not for anybody else's eyes.

In every other aspect of my life, I was a complete nightmare to be around, but as soon as I had a pen in my hand and a fresh piece of paper, something cleared, almost like when the clouds broke apart and let a stream of sunshine peek through. I was the sunshine in that analogy, in case you were wondering.

I pivoted—just like Ross from *Friends* told me to— and took a step out of the meeting room.

"My nose in the drawing is a little off, by the way," he called out.

Shit.

Chapter 3

CONFESSION #9: I TRIED TO JUMP OVER A STICK IN SKATES, MISSED, FELL OVER, AND ROLLED DOWN A HILL—INJURIES INCLUDED A CHIPPED TOOTH.

"Cousin!" I heard her before I saw her.

I whipped my head around, spotted her bright-blue hair across the bar, and lunged into a standing position.

"Ella!"

We impacted like two trucks, air rushing out of both our chests at the collision, but we didn't let go as we squeezed the life out of each other. We gently swayed left and right and broke out into a full-on dance, our arms still wrapped around each other.

"I missed your frizzy hair!" she squealed down my ear.

"And I missed your big feet!" I shouted back, pulling away.

"Ugh, look at you. You look so…*normal.*"

I scoffed at her assessment. I may have looked "normal" but I was far from it. I was a weirdo, but I wore the badge with pride.

"And you look like Marge Simpson." I raised a brow, and we both burst out laughing.

She pulled me in for another hug, this one not lasting

as long as before. It had been four years since we'd shared the same college dorm room and I missed her like crazy. I thought she was out of her mind when she first decided to move to New York after graduating, but I understood why now. She wanted to start a new life where there was nothing to remind her of growing up. That and she hated the sun. Ella was a hermit, through and through.

She yanked me back toward the bar where I had been nursing my drink. "I'll have a screaming orgasm," she told the bartender, turned around and scrunched up her nose at my drink. "Why the hell are you drinking beer?"

I lifted the bottle to my lips and took a pull. "I have work tomorrow."

She pouted as her drink was placed in front of her. "I'm so glad I can work whatever hours I want."

I nodded in acknowledgment. Ella was a graphic designer who worked from her apartment. I knew for a fact she pulled twenty-hour days sometimes, so the whole "setting your own hours" thing wasn't as great as she made it sound.

"I can't believe you've been here for well over a week and I'm only just now seeing you."

"I know." I plunked my beer down. "Work is ridiculous, I actually have to do stuff." I rolled my eyes. "And my desk is right in front of the CEO's office. It's a nightmare."

"Uh-huh." She smirked at me, and I knew what was coming before she— "How many disasters have you had so far?"

"Ugh, don't even get me started. On the first day, I ripped my skirt and had to walk around with safety pins holding it together, then tore my feet to shreds from my new heels. On my second day, I managed to spill coffee all over the tablet I was given. Then today, I tripped over my own feet as I walked into a stall in the bathroom. My head went right into the toilet bowl, soaking not only my hair but my blouse, which, to add to my embarrassment, made it see-through."

"Oh, God, I see nothing's changed."

"Nope." I shook my head, swallowing another mouthful of beer and told her, "I can only stay for one drink. I have a shit ton of work to do before tomorrow."

"What?" Her brown eyes widened, her blue, curly hair batting back and forth as she shook her head at me. "No way, you're staying for at least another two beers and three shots."

"El—"

"Don't 'Ella' me," she reprimanded, pointing at my chest. "I haven't seen you since college graduation four years ago. It's been way too long." She pushed her bottom lip out and batted her eyelashes. She knew I couldn't say no to those puppy-dog eyes. Goddamn traitor.

"Fine!" I threw my hands up in the air. "But we have to be sensible, not do a repeat of graduation night."

Her lips spread into an evil smirk. She twirled around, and she shouted, "Four shots of tequila!"

Shitballs. She was bringing out the big guns.

———

I moved my neck side to side and waved my arms about as "I'm Sexy and I Know It" blasted through the speakers of the bar. Ella was dancing like a maniac. My brows lifted as she threw her head back with some hip-thrust action and slapped her hand on an invisible ass. She did a little jump-and-shuffle move until she maneuvered through the crowd and halted behind me.

The room spun. My fourth shot of tequila continued to burn my tongue and warm my belly. It was fair to say the tipsy train came and went, and I jumped headfirst onto the wasted platform.

The song switched to the classic "Fire Burning" by Sean Kingston, and Ella squealed into my ear, "I love this song!"

"Me, too!"

I twirled around, and we both shouted the lyrics, our tone completely off as sweat rolled down our faces from the exertion of jumping around like a couple of toddlers who just ate a giant tub of candy.

The makeshift dance floor was empty, apart from us, and when I swiveled in a circle with my hands over my head, I sensed that we were being watched. Any other time—like maybe when I was sober—I'd be embarrassed, but right now I didn't give a flying fuck.

Nothing mattered. Not having to get up at six in the morning, not knowing I was going to have a hangover—nothing, because I was having the most fun I'd had since...well, since I last saw Ella. We were plunged into silence as the song finished, and I stopped to catch my breath before the next one came on. Ella disappeared, but she returned a few minutes later with a shot.

"Last one," I told her.

I expected her to ignore me, but she nodded in agreement. I licked the salt off my hand, took the shot, and clamped the slice of lime between my teeth. The tart juice flowed over my tongue, and I shuddered in relief as it extinguished the tequila's fire.

Ella removed the shot glass from me and shouted, "I wuv you, you dnow dat? It's been long time!"

I giggled at her slurred words. "Awww, I love you, too!"

We embraced each other like long-lost lovers, swaying on the dance floor. We were barefoot, yet if we weren't absolutely wasted, we'd never do such a thing. She pulled back and held up her cell. "I'll call Chad... ride." She jabbed her finger on the screen several times and finally pressed it to her ear.

I nodded as "Where Them Girls At" by David Guetta blasted out of the speakers. I did a little hop and jump. This was my favorite song right now! I started body popping, throwing my limbs in every direction, as I watched Ella talk on her cell. Her lips pulled up into a giant smile and, for a second, I was jealous that she'd found the love of her life—her words, not mine.

A flush marred her cheeks, and it jarred me, causing my leg to slip from underneath me. Ella never blushed, she was the most confident person I knew. Her gaze caught mine at that exact moment, her eyes widened, and she thrust up her hand in the international "stop" sign.

"Vi!"

I shifted to the left, trying to prevent myself from landing like a sack of potatoes on my back, but that was the biggest mistake I could have made.

I could see it happening before it did, and I went down like a two-hundred-eighty-pound fighter who had just been knocked out. My neck and shoulder smacked the thick, wooden edge of the table with so much force it made my breath catch.

I reached out, attempting to lessen the impact, but it

didn't help. My body hit the dirty bar floor, and a resounding *thud* echoed in my head. The air was ripped from my lungs. I closed my eyes and lay spread-eagled on the floor, concentrating on my breathing. I tried to take stock of my injuries as I opened my eyes. Ella was standing above me, her eyes wide and shocked.

"Are you okay?"

I groaned and rolled my head to the side as my cheeks burned. "Did anyone see?"

"Oh, God, Vi. Really?"

Ella's brows raised at my answer and her lips slowly morphed into a grin. I could see she was trying to contain herself, and I knew she wouldn't be able to hold the laughter in that was sure to burst out any second.

"What?" I asked, confused.

"You just had an epic fall, and that's what you ask?"

"I didn't fall." I placed my hand on the cold floor and grimaced at the stickiness that coated my palm. "The table attacked me."

A noise sounded in the back of Ella's throat. "I can't even…" I flicked my gaze to her face, noting how she was rolling her lips between her teeth.

"Go on." I groaned, knowing I had to get up off this dirty floor even in my drunken state. There was no way this was hygienic in any way, shape, or form. "Let it out."

This wasn't the first time Ella had witnessed one of my "klutzy moments." She'd been there for almost all of them, and although I knew she'd always help me recover, I also knew she needed to let out the laughter bubbling up inside her before she could assist my ass to the nearest emergency room.

"I…erm." She gurgled, and when I raised my brow,

she finally let it out. She threw her head back, her laughter louder than the music playing through the speakers. I turned my head to the left to look at the offending table and was greeted by three guys sitting around it with varying degrees of shock written on their faces.

"Three hours! That's all it took!" She stumbled and wiped away the tears rolling down her cheeks. The tequila was obviously taking effect.

I propped myself up on my elbows and winced at the throbbing pain in my neck and shoulder. That would hurt in the morning.

Ella's laughter turned to small chuckles, and she leaned on the table. Her weight caused it to wobble, and a glass skittered over the smooth surface. My vision was blurred, and the room moved in slow motion, so it felt as if the glass teetered on the edge of the table for eons. But I was yanked out of my slow, alcohol-fueled brain when the glass toppled over and ice-cold, sticky beer splashed me in the face and soaked through my top making me smell even worse than I already did.

Fuck my life and my stupid limbs.

Chapter 4

CONFESSION #56: I SNEEZED IN MY CRUSH'S FACE.

I walked gingerly into the small break room, and my hands shook as I reached for the refrigerator handle. I pulled the door open, wincing at the reverberations it sent up my arm, shoulder, and neck, but in spite of the tenderness, I forced myself to grab a bottle of water. I pressed the cold plastic to my cheek, sighed, and wiggled my toes, grateful for the fluffy socks cradling my sore feet. There was no way I could handle wearing my heels all day today, especially not after last night.

I didn't remember anything after I was covered with drinks. I woke up this morning in a lot of pain with a monster hangover and a craving for a slice of pizza—all signs of a good night.

Everything took twice as long when I got ready, but I still made it to work on time. Now it was just after 3:00 p.m. The throbbing in my shoulder was unbearable, but I dared not say anything to Mr. Taylor because he had two meetings this afternoon that he needed me to attend. One of which was the meeting I'd managed to rearrange after they canceled. I'd worked my ass off to get that meeting, and nothing would stop me from being there.

I made it back to my desk and let out a deep breath as I sat back in my chair. I slowly reached into my purse for some painkillers, popped four into my mouth, and glugged some water to wash them down. I groaned and twisted the lid back on the bottle.

When I spotted Mr. Taylor standing and grabbing his suit jacket, I did the same. I picked up my tablet while holding my left arm against my middle because it hurt like a bitch to keep it by my side.

He was silent as he exited his office. His gaze flicked to me, and he tilted his head, indicating I should follow him. I trailed behind him slowly and entered the elevator, riding up one floor to the conference rooms.

This floor was much the same as the one below, only not as many offices were on this one as there were six large conference rooms taking up a lot of the space. We headed to the first conference room, and two men and a woman were already seated waiting for us.

I recognized their faces right away having researched the company to within an inch of my life. I knew that they all owned an equal share and that one of them didn't want to sell and was holding everything up. But I was confident that what I had found out could be a game changer and put Mr. Taylor firmly in the running for acquiring the company.

We all shook hands, and then I sat in the seat next to Mr. Taylor. I placed my tablet in front of me and opened up the notes app.

"Thanks for taking this meeting," Mr. Taylor started.

The guy who I knew didn't want to sell grumbled, and I shot him a wide smile, trying my hardest to push through the pain rolling over my shoulder and collarbone.

"Mr. Johnson?" My voice came out confident, but I felt nothing close to it. I was taking a leap by speaking out, but I knew if I didn't, there was no way he would consider this sale. "Can I just say that the company you've built is amazing?"

His brows raised as he leaned forward.

"I was looking into it, and the amount of lives you've changed is honorable."

It was so quiet you could hear a pin drop in the room, and then he said, "That was my mission."

I nodded and turned my face slightly, spotting Mr. Taylor's puzzled look.

"And that's the reason why I won't sell to someone like you who will break it down and put thousands of people out of work."

"You don't—"

I placed my hand over Mr. Taylor's forearm to stop him and felt the muscle tense. "May I show you something?"

No one answered, so I stood, walked over to the head of the table, and clicked on the monitor to allow the big screen to come to life. I'd prepared my ass off for this meeting, determined to show everyone that I was much more than just someone who answered calls. Just because I got bored super-fast didn't mean I couldn't use my degree.

My presentation came on the screen, and I picked up the small device to control it. "I understand that your main concern is letting down your employees, but with our proposal, we wouldn't be putting one person out of work."

I clicked the button and noted how Mr. Taylor leaned forward, watching me with keen eyes. It was the presentation that he'd been working on. I knew it was only for his eyes, but we had to do something drastic otherwise Mr. Johnson would never sell, and it was ultimately him who had the final say.

"Our plan would be to split the company into different sections and make several smaller ones." I stepped forward. "This would mean *more* jobs, not less."

I paused and looked at Mr. Taylor, my eyes wide. This was where he was meant to step in, and for point two of a second, I feared he wouldn't. His brows were drawn down, the confusion on his face evident. And then it was gone, replaced by the confident smile as he stood.

"What Miss Scott is saying is true." He walked closer to me, standing shoulder to shoulder. He was so close I could feel the heat coming off his body. "When I started Taylor Industries, I wanted to create jobs, not destroy them. My goal is to offer more employment, and that's what I want to do with your company. I have the funds waiting to do this." He took a breath, shuffled closer to me, and held his hand out.

I frowned down at it and then glanced up at him. What was he trying to say? His hand touched my arm, his fingers trailing over my wrist. My breath halted in my chest, goose bumps flaring over my skin until he stopped at my palm and pulled the small device that controlled the screen out.

"You can sit down now," he whispered.

I nodded and strode back to my seat, sitting down slowly so I didn't jar my shoulder.

I was captivated for the next sixty minutes by his

speech, and when they shook hands at the end of the meeting with a promise of a second one, I wanted to jump up and down and punch the air with my fist.

They exited the room, and I turned to face Mr. Taylor who was standing a few feet away, grinning like a fool.

"I love closing deals."

"I can tell," I stated, standing and gritting my teeth from the throbbing pain in my shoulder.

He frowned down at me, and I swallowed at the intensity. When he gave a person his full attention, it was jarring and almost too much. There was an urge to both look away and beg him not to stop staring.

His frown slowly dissipated as he continued to stare, and when his gaze flicked all over my face, I bit my bottom lip. He zoned in on the action, and the muscles in his neck tensed. He watched me for a beat longer and then took a step back.

"You did well today." He rubbed the back of his neck and cleared his throat. "I had no idea you could do that." He paused. "Thank you."

"You're welcome." I smiled, and my stomach fluttered. It was plain as day to see how much he loved the company he'd built with his own two hands, and the way he talked about getting people into work and creating an environment that people enjoy was fascinating.

He tilted his head toward the door. "We have a meeting with the head of departments." He didn't make a move.

"I know," I whispered, afraid to talk too loudly.

What the hell was going on? Was my boss giving me the eye? Because I was definitely giving it to him.

"We should…erm…"

He focused those dark-blue eyes back on me, a rainbow of emotions running through them. But the moment was gone almost as soon as it started. He shuttered it off, spun around, and headed out the door, leaving me to follow.

That was...

I'd never been so turned on and in so much pain all at the same time, and I had no idea what to do or say, so I followed him to the conference room two doors down.

Everyone was waiting when I walked inside a couple of seconds after him. He sat at the head of the table and tilted his head, indicating that I should take the position on his left. I slid into the chair, but he didn't acknowledge me as he addressed the staff with business details, asking for updates from each department.

Once we got to the man who was sitting to my left, I felt a bead of sweat running down my temple. Even shuffling on the seat was too much pain for me to handle. I didn't think I'd ever been in this much agony before. Not when I broke my ankle skipping, not when I rode down a hill on my bike and the front wheel got caught in a rabbit hole and I flew over the handlebars, dislocating my shoulder. And not even the time I stumbled into the side mirror of a car and broke my cheekbone.

"We have two more companies we could split apart and—"

"Fuck," I spat when the guy beside me leaned over, handing Mr. Taylor a folder and hitting my shoulder. My neck, shoulder, and everything in between throbbed, and it was pure torture, so much so I felt tears stinging the backs of my eyes as all gazes swung my way. "I'm sorry," I choked out, my voice barely audible.

I didn't want to chance a glance at Mr. Taylor, so I kept my head down as much as I could bear as the man beside me cleared his throat and continued. But when I glanced up, Mr. Taylor's gaze was fixed on me, searching, probing, looking for something.

I tried to mask the pain I was in, but he must have seen it because five minutes later, he was declaring the meeting finished.

"Miss Scott," he boomed, his voice cutting through all the murmuring voices in the room. "My office...*now*."

Swallowing against my dry throat, I closed my eyes and prepared to stand. When I did, I gritted my teeth against the white-hot sensation rolling through me. I followed him, back into the elevator and into his office.

A muscle in his jaw pulsated much like the music in the bar last night. He stopped at his office door and waited for me to enter first. I maneuvered past him, and he shut the door with a click.

"Sit down," his rough voice commanded.

I shuffled over to one of the chairs opposite his desk and slowly lowered myself, my breath catching when my elbow touched the side of the leather.

He sat down behind his desk and watched me for several seconds. His eyes narrowed as he took me all in, exploring my eyes, my neck, and my breasts. His gaze settled there, and I was hyperaware of my nipples as they scraped against the soft fabric of my blouse with each lungful of air I expelled. I licked my lips at the precise moment he moved his attention to my mouth.

"What the hell was that?" he growled, but he didn't give me a chance to answer. "A meeting with all the department heads, and you think it's appropriate to curse?"

"I—"

"I should have known the first day you wouldn't be any good. You haven't even finished my schedule or—"

"Yes, I have," I interrupted, not caring about his stupid rules. My pulse pounded in my ears at his dismissive tone. I'd gone above and beyond researching for the meeting this afternoon so I could prove I wasn't just here to answer his phone and schedule dates in his calendar. I narrowed my eyes and flattened my lips into a straight line. "It's in your inbox. I sent it the first day."

He raised a brow at me and clicked the mouse next to his computer. After several seconds he said, "It's not here."

Huffing out a breath, I stood and slowly walked over to him, just now realizing I still had my fluffy socks on. *Shit.*

Trying not to bring attention to them, I moved in beside him, staring at the screen. I pulled in a lungful of air, hating that all I could smell was his addictive cologne.

"There." I pointed with my good hand at the screen. "Viloveschocolateforlife@taylorindustries.com."

"You…what?" He shook his head, clicked on the email, and opened up the attachment. It popped up and filled the screen, all the color coding he wanted in place. "Right, okay." I raised my brow, not expecting an apology, but Jesus Christ, he was an asshole. "That still doesn't excuse the cursing."

"He bumped me," I tried to defend.

He looked away from his computer, leaning back slightly to stare at me. My lips parted as his head came level with my chest. I hoped to God my nipples weren't spearheading in his direction, but I knew if I checked, he'd see me.

"So?"

Blowing out a breath, I turned around to put some distance between us, and leaned my ass against his desk, ignoring the scolding look he gave me.

"I went out last night and—"

"Good for you, but that has no relevance at all with—"

"I saw my cousin—"

"Stop interrupting me," he boomed, a pinched expression on his face.

I rolled my eyes and gave him an incredulous stare. "*You're* interrupting *me*." His jaw flexed as he clenched his teeth. I took it as my cue to continue. "As I was saying, I went out with my cousin, who I haven't seen in years. One thing led to another and many tequilas later, I'm dancing."

"What does this have to do with—"

"You should know," I stated. "I'm accident prone. I fall over my own two feet and don't have a day where something embarrassing doesn't happen to me." I shrugged my good shoulder, which was a *giant* mistake. But I worked through it as I told him, "I've learned to live with it."

I pulled in a stuttering breath and winced at the throb it caused. I opened my mouth to tell him the rest when he pushed his chair back and stood.

"Why are you pulling that face?"

I gulped. "I fell over and hit my shoulder and neck on the edge of a table before my cousin made drinks topple onto me. I don't remember much after that—

apart from waking up this morning with a hangover and in agony."

He took two steps toward me causing his body to be only inches away from mine. He towered over me in the most delicious way and my thoughts went haywire with him being so close.

My legs parted slightly, almost as if they were begging him to slip between them. It felt natural to want him to move closer, and all I could think about is what he would do if he did. Would his smooth palm caress the side of my neck in the same way it had over the back of my knee in the elevator only days ago? I licked my lips and felt my cheeks heat.

"Where does it hurt?" he asked, his deep voice softer this time. I set my gaze on him and witnessed the concern flashing in his eyes. I stayed silent. "Tell me where it hurts, Violet."

Why did my name sound so good rolling off his tongue? I stared at him, willing him to say it again so I could lock the memory away and bring it out when I needed to—

"Violet."

"I...here." I pointed where the pain was the worst.

"Can..." He cleared his throat and tilted his head at my collarbone. "Can I check?"

Rolling my lips between my teeth, I wanted to tell him no but what came out of my mouth was, "Yes."

I undid the first two buttons of my blouse and tried to pull it aside. "Shit on a stick! That fucking hurts."

He gripped the edge of the pastel-pink material. "Jesus Christ," he spat out and ran the pads of his fingers over my collarbone. I wanted to savor his touch, but it hurt like a mothertrucker. "I think you've broken it."

"Not again," I groaned, but I already knew what it looked like. I'd examined it closely when I got ready for work this morning. The purple bruise and lump were more than enough to tell me what I'd done. I'd just hoped that if I ignored it for a while that maybe it would go away.

How stupid was that?

My stomach rolled when his finger trailed over what I was sure was the lump, and my body swayed backward.

"Hey, *hey*." His hands cupped my face, bringing my attention back to him.

"I'm sorry," I croaked, those earlier tears coming back and rolling down my cheeks, making a path over his hands. "I'm such a klutz, and now you're probably going to fire me, and I have the worst insurance because of how many times I've been in the hospital. I won't be able to pay my medical bills, which means I'm going to have to call my dad and tell him I've broken another bone—what... What are you doing?"

He stepped back and slipped on his suit jacket, all the while his gaze trained on me. He flared his nostrils, shook his head, and stepped around his desk. I was enthralled with each of his movements, and couldn't take my eyes off him as exited his office, gathered my things, and stalked back toward me.

"I'm taking you to the hospital." He helped me into my coat. "Where's your winter coat?"

"This *is* my winter coat." He frowned, a V forming between his brows. My hand moved before I could register, and I tried to smooth the V out. "You shouldn't do that. You'll get wrinkles."

His lips lifted into a smirk as he grasped my hand. The heat of his fingers seeped into my skin, warming me and momentarily made me forget about the pain.

He led me out of his office, stopped at the main reception desk, and dropped my hand as he told the woman at the front desk, "Field my calls. If it's important, call me. If not, then it can wait until Monday."

"What—"

He turned back around, sauntered away from her, and punched the elevator button. The faintest warmth of his hand skimmed across my lower back as we stepped inside. The doors closed, leaving us in the confined space once again, only this time it felt different, like something happened in his office that had him seeing me as more than the person sent from LA to cover for his PA. *Oh, hey! That rhymed! I'm a poet and I didn't even—*

"Violet?"

"Hmmm?" I blinked and locked my gaze onto his wide, blue eyes. I was adrift, unsure if the butterflies dancing in my stomach were due to the drop of the elevator or some sort of electricity sparking between us.

"What the hell are those on your feet?"

The electricity died. The butterflies stopped dancing. *Shit.*

———

I waited on the edge of the hospital bed, my feet dangling off the side and not touching the floor, with a silly grin on my face. *Morphine was the best.*

We'd been here for three hours, and Mr. Taylor was

sitting in a chair beside me with his face buried in his cell. He looked up every now and again, flashed me a closed-lip smile, and then moved his attention back to his cell. He didn't speak another word while Jeeves brought us here, and except to ask me my personal check-in information at the reception desk when we arrived, he hadn't spoken to me since we were at the office.

He stayed in the small, curtained-off area while I got an X-ray, and now we were waiting for the results of said X-ray.

I grabbed my stomach as it growled loudly, earning me a smirk from Mr. Taylor. He shuffled forward on the chair and opened his mouth just as the curtain opened. A man in light-blue scrubs and a white jacket entered the room, holding an electronic tablet. He glanced up and his gaze skirted across me and over to Mr. Taylor, then he whipped the curtain closed and cleared his throat.

"Miss Scott, I—"

"Violet," I told him, a giggle working its way up my throat. What the hell was wrong with me? I never giggled. "Like the color."

He chuckled under his breath and swiped his finger along the device screen, bringing something up and turning it to face me. "You have a broken collarbone."

I leaned closer to the screen. "Ugh. I thought so."

He lowered the tablet. "Can you tell me how you did this?"

I retold the story while he watched me intently, his gaze briefly moving over to Mr. Taylor. "I've examined all your records, and it seems this is one of many broken bones you've had over the last few years."

My eyes fluttered closed. I knew what's coming.

Every time I visited an ER with a broken bone, they saw all the other times I'd come in and assumed there was something else to it.

"Uh-huh," I answered, opening my eyes back up. "Look, I know what you're going to say, and to be honest, I'm so hungry right now I can't be bothered to explain to you how accident prone I am. I need food, preferably pizza. Oh! And could I get some more of those awesome pain meds?"

"I—"

"Look, Doc, I just really want to go home, eat, and then get a good night's sleep." I waved my hand in the air. "Fix me up and send me away."

"Right, well..." His dark-brown gaze flicked to Mr. Taylor again and he shuffled on the spot. "We'll be applying a figure-of-eight brace with an arm sling for immobilization, which you'll need to wear for the next six weeks or so. The nurse will give you a referral list of orthopedic specialists in the area. They will determine the specific timeframe for the brace and sling use, and revise your treatment plan accordingly." He glanced at the tablet again. "I'll also prescribe you some pain medication for a couple of days. After that, over-the-counter medication will work just as well."

He placed the tablet onto the small, rolling table at the end of the bed and typed away. All the while all I could think about was the amount of money all of this would cost me. I wondered if seeing a specialist would be covered by the health insurance attached to the job? I could only hope it would otherwise I was fucked—figuratively not literally. Although that sounded like heaven too. When was the last time I'd had some bow-chicka-wow-wow?

Too freaking long.

The curtain opened, and this time a nurse entered. Her honey-colored eyes crinkled at the corners as she lifted her lips into a smile.

"Violet, this is Nurse Aliyah. She'll be applying the brace for you as well as giving you that referral list. You'll need to—"

The beeping of his pager cut him off, and when he glanced down and read what was on there, he rushed out of the room.

"Looks like you've been in the wars," the nurse commented, not acknowledging the doctor's quick exit.

"You can say that again." My tone was light and airy, but I felt anything but. It didn't matter how many times I'd been in the ER, it never felt good. I just wanted to get out of the sterile room and into the large comfortable bed back at the hotel.

The nurse strode forward. "You will need to remove your blouse."

"My blouse?" I asked at the same time that Mr. Taylor stood and moved a step closer.

"The best option is to wear the brace under your clothes," the nurse explained. "Immobilization is key with a fracture like this and wearing just a sling won't do the job as good or fast as this."

I slowly reached for the first button on my blouse and winced, the morphine having started to wear off. This morning when I woke up, I knew I couldn't push my arm through one of my pullover blouses, so I wore this button-up one.

I tried to get the small button out of the hole, but after what felt like a lifetime, Mr. Taylor asked, "Do you want me to help?"

Looking up at him, I got lost in his blue eyes. I should have been mortified, I should have wanted to ask him to leave and not see me at my most vulnerable, but the earnest expression on his face had me nodding my head.

His large hands reached forward, and that's when I realized I didn't have a bra on. "Wait. I erm... I..." I glanced between Mr. Taylor and the nurse. How could something like this embarrass me yet breaking my collarbone by falling over didn't?

"Vi." Mr. Taylor paused. "Let's get this on, and then we can head home. Come on, it won't take long." I was surprised at the softness in his voice.

"But—"

"Your partner will also need to know how it's applied so he can help you put it back on after showering—which is the only time you can take it off."

"He's not—"

"Let's get this on and then you can get on your way," the nurse interrupted at the same time that Mr. Taylor undid the first button.

I squeezed my eyes closed, wondering several things at once: Why didn't he correct the nurse? How was I going to get this back on after I had a shower? And why the heck was he being so nice to me? He should have fired me by now and told me to go back to LA, yet he hadn't. He was standing there, undoing my second and third button, while I waited for my boobs to spring free and announce themselves. *Hey, world! Look at me! I'm free and not contained in a torture device people like to call a bra!*

They loved the freedom, and I was sure right now they were rejoicing in the fact that I probably wouldn't contain them for the next month or so. I just hoped people didn't get offended when my nips popped out to say hello at the most inopportune times.

"Fuck me," Mr. Taylor groaned, and that was the point my eyelids sprang open.

"I tried to tell you," I whispered, my voice breaking. My boss was staring at my boobs. Shitting hell.

"I…" His Adam's apple bobbed as he swallowed. He tore his gaze away from my chest and moved his attention to my face. He studied me, and I was sure he could see the tears pushing forward, glassing up my eyes. I was never going to be able to look at him again after this.

"It's okay," he finally said, gazing back down and undoing the next few buttons with lightning speed. "How do you put it on?" he asked the nurse, not moving from where he'd maneuvered himself to block my chest.

"I'll slip one arm in, then I need to adjust the back in order to get the other arm in and tighten the brace completely," the nurse replied.

Mr. Taylor nodded, pushed the blouse off my shoulders, gathered it and held it against my chest to cover me. He shifted to the side, his large palm covering my breast, one of his fingertips brushing over my nipple and causing a shiver to roll through me.

His blue eyes met mine, darkening as his gaze dipped to where his hand was. I heard his small growl, and the noise made me even more…*excited*. I couldn't look away from his hypnotizing eyes, and all I wanted was to push myself into his warm palm.

He shifted closer to me. It was a small movement, but I noticed it, hyperaware of his body and mine. The nurse pushed one part of the brace up my bad arm and placed it on the ball of my shoulder. It broke Mr. Taylor and me out of the connection we had. We both glanced away as the nurse went around the other side of the bed and slid the straps up my good arm. All the while, she was coaching Mr. Taylor on how to do it. I should have been paying attention, too, because I was the one who was going to have to figure out how to do this on my own, but I couldn't because all I could focus on was his hand on my chest, his finger moving back and forth. I didn't even think he was aware he was doing it now.

"Ballbags!" I shouted when the brace was tightened, pulling my shoulders back.

"This is the position it needs to be in. I'll mark the brace so you know how far to tighten it."

I didn't listen to the rest of what she said because my head was spinning and my empty stomach rolled. I was going to be sick, I could feel it. Or was I going to pass out? I felt hot and then cold, my clammy skin sticky.

I had to get out of here. I needed painkillers and my bed.

"Thank you," I heard Mr. Taylor say and then the curtain was moved aside, and my blouse was being pulled away from my chest, my arms being slipped through it, and the buttons fastened.

He was methodical in his ministrations, and I finally plucked the courage to look at him when he finished dressing me. His thumb pressed on the screen of his cell, and he brought it up to his ear. "We're leaving now, Jeeves." He ended the call and focused on me.

"I bet you didn't think you'd see my boobs when you woke up this morning, huh?"

He chuckled, the sound deep and rich. It made me want to climb into his body and press repeat over and over again so I could bask in it. He shrugged. "I've learned one thing over the last week."

"Oh, yeah?" I asked, letting him help me down off the bed.

"Yeah." He wrapped my coat around me, gathered his things, and plucked a piece of paper up off the bed. His warm hand caressed the bottom of my back as he pulled the curtain aside. "No two days are the same with you around." He led me through the ER and toward the main doors.

"You can say that again. My life is full of surprises. I never know what's coming, but at least it's fun. Well, not the pain aspect, or the falling over, or the jobs I've been fired from."

He raised a brow as we exited the hospital. "How many jobs have you been fired from?"

"Erm…well, six in the last seven months?" I voiced it like a question. A tired breath left my throat as we walked toward the idling car Jeeves was sitting in. "Seven, if you count this one."

I felt the loss of Mr. Taylor's hand as he pulled his palm off the bottom of my back. He opened the back door for me and smiled. The kind of smile that a child gave their dad when he let them have a piece of candy before dinner. My heart raced in my chest, and right then I decided I'd do all I could to get another one of those smiles from him.

I slowly got into the car, careful not to jostle my body.

He closed the door, walked around to the other side, and slid in next to me. "This job?"

Jeeves pulled away from the entrance, and I looked

over at Mr. Taylor. "Well, yeah. You won't want to keep me—"

"Vi, I'm not firing you. You can have a few days off and then come back. I need a PA right now, and I don't have time to find another one. You only need one hand to answer a phone and type for now. It may take longer, but..." His eyes flashed as they dipped to my chest again. "I'm not going to fire you."

"You're not?" I asked, my voice vulnerable. *I'm never vulnerable.*

"No." He shook his head, a smirk lifting up the corners of his lips. "I may have to get a giant roll of Bubble Wrap to encase you in, though."

I laughed. "I tried it once," I told him.

"You tried it?"

"Mmm-hmm. I was twelve and, during the year previous, I'd broken my wrist, dislocated my shoulder, sprained my ankle, given myself two black eyes and numerous cuts and scrapes. So, I decided to try it."

When I glanced up at him, I witnessed the laughter behind his eyes as he asked, "What did you do while trying the Bubble Wrap out?"

I let out a long breath and whispered, "I knocked myself out. I fell and couldn't save myself, and I hit my head against a brick wall."

Chapter 5

CONFESSION #81: I SLIPPED ON A BANANA SKIN... AN ACTUAL BANANA SKIN!

Ella: You did what?!

Me: I broke my collarbone.

Ella: And you still went to work?

Ella: Guuurrl, you cray cray.

Ella: This is what happens when you mix Alcohol and Vi.

Ella: You become even more dangerous…if that's even possible.

There were two kinds of texters in the world: the kind who fit all they wanted to say into one message, and then the kind who broke it up into ten separate messages. Ella was the latter. Why couldn't she just fit it all into one message?

Me: I know!! Then my new boss took me to the hospital.

Ella: Oh, snap!!

Me: In the room with me…without a bra on…

Ella: Vi! Tell me you showed him the goods!

Ella: Is he hot?

Me: Yes, to both, but it has no relevance to the fact I can't get this goddamn contraption on! I messaged you for help!!

Ella: Laughing so hard I'm crying over here.

Ella: I'm sorry. I really can't get there, Chad has taken us to his parents for the week.

Shit. Shit, shit, shit!

I stared down at the brace in my hand then up at myself in the mirror. I looked like I had a pair of grocery bags under my eyes and my hair was wet and limp. Why had I thought this was a good idea? *Because I needed a goddamn shower, that's why!*

It was Sunday afternoon. After we got back from the hospital with my prescription, I headed to my room, intent on sleeping the next couple of days away. I only woke up on Saturday to order room service, but I fell asleep while a movie played on the TV.

A day and a half later, and I needed a shower like my life depended on it.

So here I was, a towel wrapped around me, pain shooting through my shoulder at every movement because I didn't have the brace on, and I had nobody around to help me.

I searched the room, spinning around in a slow circle as if something in here may help me solve my problem. Toilet-paper holder, towels, sink, fancy hotel soap…toilet brush. I could safely say none of those things would help me.

Ella: If your boss was taught how to put it on then ask him, Vi.

Ella: I know you don't want to…stop pulling a face! It's the only way!

Ella: I'll come visit when I get back on Friday. Chad needs to talk to his brother anyway, and he stays in the same hotel as you, so I'll come over and we can drink some wine, k?

Blowing out a deep breath, I shot off a text to her to say we'll meet on Friday as I headed back toward the bedroom.

I sat down on the edge of the unmade bed and wrinkled my nose up at the dirty sheets. Maybe El was right? The only way I was going to get this thing back on was by calling Mr. Taylor and asking him to help me.

Was I really going to do this?

I'd known him for a couple of weeks, and in that span of time I'd cursed in front of him because of stupid heels, had him look at me like I was an alien when he heard about the toilet incident, and now this—I showed him my boobs!

He'd seen them once, so another time wouldn't hurt, right?

I picked my cell back up, scrolled down to his name, clicked on it, and brought it to my ear with a wince.

I couldn't believe I was doing this.

It rang and rang as I watched the small clock on the bedside table, noting I had an hour before I could take my next lot of painkillers. After the fifth attempt, I stood, wondering what I was meant to do now. *He lived at the hotel!* They'd know where he was. Why hadn't I thought of that before?

I grabbed some pajama shorts and wiggled them on using my good arm. Sweat marred my brow. It was too much, so as soon as they were on, I blew my hair out of my face and pulled the towel tighter. I knew if I tried to get a top on right now I'd just be hurting myself even more. *No, thank you.*

I pulled the door open to my room and looked left and right. Seeing no one, I stepped out and walked as fast as I could toward the elevators without hurting myself more. Jamming my finger on the button, I willed the elevator to move faster as I checked around the hallway as if there could be someone waiting to jump on me at any second.

The doors whooshed open and I practically jumped inside and slammed my hand down on the ground floor button. I stared at the numbers over the top of the doors and only then realized I was still holding my brace in my hand. As if the next person I came across would be able to put it on for me.

The elevator stopped, and I stepped out into the

main foyer. It was empty apart from the doorman who did a double take when he spotted me.

I moved toward the woman sitting behind the reception desk.

"I...erm..." *Get your words out, Vi.* "Hi!" The loudness of my voice jarred not only the woman staring at me with wide eyes but myself too. Leaning against the desk, I tried my hardest to look normal. Normal being a relative word. "I was wondering if you know where Mr. Taylor is."

"Mr. Taylor?" she asked, her face a mask of surprise.

"Yeah, I'm his PA, and there's a matter of...utter importance he must attend to immediately." I laughed, but it wasn't humorous, more like it came from someone who lived in crazy town. "As you can see," I said, waving my arm at myself. "I came straight down here."

"I...he's attending a meeting in the main room."

"Awesome." I twirled around. "Thanks!"

"You may not want to go..." Her voice trailed off as I pulled open the doors, my lips lifting into a smile but dying down when I saw what was in this room.

There had to be at least thirty people, all dressed in cocktail dresses and suits, and then there was me—in a towel, my hair wet, a brace in my hand. *Fuckadoodledoo.*

No one had noticed me yet, so I started to turn around, but before I even made it one step, the resounding crack of the door slamming closed reverberated off the walls. Everyone's talking and laughter died off, the silence surrounding me as I felt all of their stares on my back.

I froze. My skin burned and all I wanted to do was cover my face with my hands and escape silently. I closed my eyes. There was no way I was going to slip out unnoticed now. I had to turn around. It was fine. It was *fine*. I could do this, it wasn't like I was naked under this towel... Well, not completely.

Turning around slowly, I swallowed and willed myself not to flinch at all the eyes focused on me. I lifted my hand holding the brace while trying to wave. "Hi."

My gaze traveled over everyone, searching for Mr. Taylor and I spotted him leaning against the bar, his eyes wide and his lips spread into a grim line. *Uh-oh.*

"I..." I stepped forward, keeping my eyes connected to his. "I have an urgent matter you need to look at." Walking toward him, I acknowledged all the people who were still watching me. "It's okay, I have clothes on underneath this." I halted in front of Mr. Taylor whispering, "Shorts at least."

"Vi," he growled, taking hold of my good arm. The heat from his fingers seeped into my bones and made me wish he was touching me elsewhere. "What are you doing?"

I moved a little closer as the murmurs started up, not wanting anyone to know why I came in here. "I tried to call you." I focused my attention on him. His pupils enlarged the longer he stared at me, and I was acutely aware of the tightening of his hand and the way his chest moved with each breath. We were in our own little bubble, and for a second I forgot why I'd come down here. "I needed...help."

His expression became void of any emotion at the word *help*.

He dropped my arm, and I bit down on my bottom lip so I wouldn't moan at the loss of contact. His eyes flashed at the motion, his tongue darting out and wetting his lips. He shook his head and pulled out his cell. "It was on silent."

I studied each one of his movements as he placed his drink on the bar and stepped toward me. My breath caught as his chest met mine, and I could feel that blush from when I first entered the room returning. I swallowed and blurted out, "I had a shower."

His gaze flicked down, and I tightened my grip on the edge of my towel. I could practically feel his eyes grazing over my cleavage, and the longer he stared, the faster my breaths became.

"I can see that." He raised a brow and held his hand out. "Come on, let's get you back upstairs and put the brace on you."

I didn't think twice about placing my hand in his, relishing in the warm, smoothness against my palm. It was both soft but rough at the same time, a complete contradiction. His large one engulfed mine, and I closed my eyes briefly as we moved through the throng of people.

He opened the door, letting go of my hand as I walked ahead of him. He grasped it again as if it was second nature and led me across the foyer. At the sound of our footsteps, the woman behind the desk looked up.

"Marla, could you let them know I had to attend to an emergency situation and I won't make it back tonight?"

"You don't have to—"

"Of course," she replied, cutting me off.

"Thanks."

His hand tightened around mine, and he moved a step toward the elevator. I yanked back on his hand but squeezed it at the same time, not willing to let go yet. I cleared my throat and asked her, "Do you think someone could come and change my sheets? I slept in them all day yesterday and..." I wrinkled my nose, trying to tell her silently they were disgusting.

"I'm sorry, Miss Scott, there's no one working housekeeping until six in the morning."

"Oh...I...okay, tomorrow will do." I gave her a sad smile.

Mr. Taylor pulled me away toward the elevator, and it opened up the exact second we got there. "You can sleep in my guest room," he said, his thumb rubbing back and forth across my knuckles as he stood beside me like we'd done this a thousand times before.

"Oh, no. It's more than okay. I mean, just because you've seen my boobs doesn't mean you have to offer me your spare bed. The sheets will be fine for one more night."

His loud laugh caught me off guard, and my head snapped up toward him, causing me to groan from the movement.

"Shit, you okay, Violet?"

"I...*no*... It hurts like a bitch." I let my back fall against the side of the elevator, releasing his hand and bracing myself as waves of pain ran through me. "I can't believe I did this to myself. I swear I'm never drinking tequila again."

He chuckled softly, his body moving closer to mine. "I've said the same thing to myself a few times, too."

"You have?" The elevator doors opened, and we walked along the hallway, back to my room. "I don't see you as the tequila type, Mr. Taylor."

I waved the card to open the door, and we both stepped inside and into the seating area of my suite.

"Axel."

I turned around, staring at him like he'd lost his mind. "Huh?"

"It's Axel." He shrugged, his gaze batting down to my chest and back up. "Like you said, I've seen your boobs, so we may as well be on a first-name basis."

"Hmmm." I tilted my head to the side, running my gaze from his brogue-covered feet, up his suit pants and over the white shirt covered with a navy jacket. "It suits you. You should keep it."

"Thanks." His lips lifted into a smirk. "I've had it for thirty years so far, I think I can get another twenty out of it at least."

I broke out into a wide grin, enjoying this side of him. It was almost as if we were normal people in a normal world where he wasn't my boss and I didn't injure myself in the most awkward of ways.

Neither of us looked away, caught in the same web as earlier, only this time there was no one else around to distract us. My skin tingled at his attention, and I was even more aware of the fact I was only wearing shorts underneath this towel.

"Give it to me."

My eyes nearly popped out of my head at his words said from only inches away from my face. His hand trailed a path over my wrist causing goose bumps to spread like wildfire. Did he just say what I thought he did?

"I... What?"

"The brace, Vi. Give it to me."

"Oh." I cleared my throat, feeling stupid for thinking he meant something else. What the hell did I think he was talking about? I had to stop the awkward laugh that bubbled up inside me as I passed the brace over. "I tried to do it myself, but I couldn't get it—"

"It's okay, I told you to call if you needed me to put it on."

"I know." I swallowed as he moved in behind me. "I did call."

He didn't comment as his hand grasped my bad arm softly. I shivered as the soft material whispered over my skin and up to my shoulder. My eyes closed and I let out a small breath as he did the same to my other arm.

"You'll have to drop the back of the towel for a second," he whispered in my ear, his breath skirting against the side of my neck.

I dropped it a little but kept it secured against my chest as he tightened the brace. I was prepared for the sensation and even more relieved when it came because the pain wasn't as bad.

His fingertips danced over my shoulders and trailed down my arms. I felt his head dipping down. "Your skin is so soft."

My teeth sunk into my bottom lip, and I was afraid I'd cause the skin to break with how hard I was biting down. "Thanks, I erm… I…" I turned my head, glancing at him out of the corner of my eyes as I blurted out, "I use lotion."

Our eyes met, our lips centimeters apart. The air around us crackled, my body growing even hotter as his attention focused solely on me. His blue eyes swirled with promises in their depths as his gaze flicked down to my lips and he moved a step forward. Licking my lips, I held my breath as he dipped his head.

He was going to kiss me, and all I could focus on was his perfect ear.

I never knew an ear could be so sexy, but I found myself reaching for it and trailing the pad of my finger around the edge. I moved my gaze from it and back to his eyes as his hand grasped my waist, squeezing gently as he murmured, "I shouldn't want to kiss you."

"You shouldn't," I whispered back.

"I should let you go and walk out of here."

I nodded, agreeing with him but hoping like hell he didn't. He'd been a distraction from the moment I laid eyes on him, but I never thought we'd be here now, two weeks later.

His other hand lifted, his thumb trailing along my bottom lip. "So soft."

I groaned, my eyes fluttering closed as I felt him move impossibly closer. *This was actually happening.* I opened my eyes and twisted around to try and face him fully. But as I did, my leg came up and I accidentally kneed him. *In the groin.*

"Fucccckk." He stumbled back, his hands cupping his junk, his eyes squeezed closed.

"Oh my God. I'm so so sorry!" I gasped as he groaned again, taking a step back and flopping down on the sofa. "I never—I—*shit.*"

He held his hand up in the international sign for stop. "Just…"

I stepped toward him but halted, not sure what I should do. Did I go to him? Leave him?

Finally, after ten minutes of watching him like he was a bomb about to explode, he stood. His eyes met mine briefly, and I tried to pull my lips up into a smile, but I knew it was more of a grimace. He limped toward the door, having mostly recovered from my attack. He halted beside me, not one part of his body touching mine. His gaze tracked across my face, shoulders, and landed back on my eyes again.

"I'm sorry," I whispered for a second time.

He was silent for a beat, emotion flashing over his eyes briefly until he locked it away. "I'll keep my cell on loud if you need me. Take tomorrow off."

Shaking my head, I said, "It's okay, I can—"

He stepped away, yanked the door open, and glanced back one last time. "Take the day off, Vi. I'll see you Tuesday morning."

The door closed behind him, the click of the lock engaging bringing me back to reality.

Was I about to kiss my boss?

Did I just knee said boss in the groin?

Did I regret not kissing him?

Yes. To all accounts.

———

I looked up from my notepad and the drawing of a crazy woman talking to her plants, and I smirked as I noted that I had basically drawn a picture of myself. I closed the pad and moved my gaze toward the barman as he stopped in front of me.

"Can I get you another?" he asked.

"Better not. I haven't had anything to eat yet." I slid off the stool and wobbled slightly. *Shit, maybe I'd had one too many beers?*

"We serve food in that section," he said, pointing to the other side of the room.

I snorted. "Yeah, I'm not paying these prices. I can't afford to go into bankruptcy."

His almost black eyes flashed with laughter as his

lips quirked. The longer I stared at him, the more I scrunched up my nose. He was good-looking in that All-American-vibe sort of way. I bet he was one of the popular guys at high school, the kind who would have laughed relentlessly when I fell over my own two feet.

Jerk. I hated him instantly.

Spinning around, I gripped my notepad, stepped toward the door to return to my room, and caught sight of a head of dark-blond hair. I shouldn't go over there, I really shouldn't.

Why were my feet moving?

It was like I wasn't in my own body. Instead, an alien had taken over, controlling all my movements and thoughts.

"Well, hello there." I inwardly winced at myself as I gripped the back of the chair opposite him, waiting for any kind of acknowledgment. He ignored me, so naturally I pulled the chair out and plonked myself down, staring as he cut his steak up and brought it to his mouth. Oh, God, maybe I should have something to eat because that looked juicy as hell—the steak and his lips, that is.

Placing my notepad on my lap, I leaned my elbow on the table and rested my chin on my palm. "Well, hello to you, too, Vi. How are you? Good? Oh, awesome. I'm good, too," I said, mocking him.

His brow quirked, but he didn't make any other movements.

"How was your day, Vi?" I continued the sarcastic conversation with myself, leaned back, and blew out a deep breath. "Well, I have a boss who is a tyrant, and I haven't stopped all day. Do you know how hard the copy machine is to work? Why the hell does it have two thousand and forty settings? Whatever happened to one button to copy the piece of paper you put in there?"

My gaze settled on his hand as it gripped the knife. "How was your day, Mr. Taylor?" I waited for him to answer. He shoved a forkful of potatoes in his mouth and chewed slowly as he stared down at the screen of his cell. Man, he was so freaking rude. I was about to push out of my chair as he scooped up another forkful, but something propelled me forward to keep talking.

"Me?" I deepened my voice, attempting to match his baritone, and his fork stopped halfway to his mouth. "I had to sit in so many meetings, being all...bossy." I rolled my eyes, puffing out my chest. "It's so tiring being the big, bad boss."

Yes! Finally, he looked at me.

I offered him a small smile, waiting for him to answer me... But he didn't.

Oh my freaking Lord.

"You know, you're kind of rude," I stated, scooping up his glass of water and taking a sip.

He gently placed his knife and fork on his plate as he leaned back, watching me.

"Talking to you is like trying to get blood out of a wall... Wait, that doesn't sound right." I frowned and glanced to the side. "Stone. Blood out of a stone."

I set the water back on the table and dragged the pad of my finger along the condensation that was gathering around the outside of the glass. "Are you gonna finish that?" I pointed at his half-eaten steak, waiting for some kind of signal from him.

He pushed it toward me and picked up his cell.

I dove for the knife and fork, wincing at the twinge in my shoulder. I really needed to remember I'd broken my collarbone. Taking a deep breath, I cut a piece off, and brought the mouth-watering steak to my lips. "Oh my God." I closed my eyes, relishing in the taste. "This is sooooo good." I parted my lips, cut another piece off, and shoved that in my mouth, too. "There must be something in the New York water because everything tastes better here. Or maybe it's because I haven't eaten all day?" I continued to devour, not bothering to look at him, knowing he probably wasn't paying attention to me, anyway. "I went to that food place a few doors down from the office today for lunch, and all they had was sushi. Obviously, you need to buy your lunch at breakfast time to get something decent. I don't want slimy, raw fish anywhere near me." I shivered, remembering the way it felt in my mouth. "All I wanted was a sandwich." I popped the last piece of steak in my mouth, set the utensils down, and leaned back, resting my hand on my stomach. "I'm so stuffed and—"

"Do you ever stop talking?"

I jumped out of my skin at his deep baritone, not expecting him to talk, and when I glanced up, he had a slight smirk on his face. Maybe he had been paying attention, after all?

"You were listening to me?" I asked, leaning toward him, my voice a mere whisper.

"How could I not?" He mimicked my action and placed his palms on the high-gloss table. "You talk a mile a minute and never shut up. Don't you get tired of hearing your own voice?"

"Sometimes." I shrugged, bringing my hands forward and knocking the plate. I flinched as the utensils clanged with so much force I was sure it would break the porcelain. The fork rolled off the table and plummeted to the floor. "Crap on a stick." I scrambled to retrieve the fork, but I banged my head underneath the table as I tried to sit back up.

"Jesus," Mr. Taylor huffed. "Can't take you anywhere."

I swallowed. "Well…" I placed the fork on the plate gently. My chair grated across the floor as I shoved back from the table and stood with my notebook clutched to my chest. "You technically didn't bring me here."

"No, you're right. I didn't. You decided to accost me while I was eating dinner and talk me to death."

I shot him a tight-lipped smile. "You're welcome." I did a weird half-bow movement and waved. "Catch you later, boss."

I made it halfway to the door before I heard his deep chuckle and my smile widened. Maybe he wasn't such an asshole, after all? I mean, he did share his steak with me, right?

Chapter 6

CONFESSION #24: I TRIED TO MATTRESS
SURF ON A SLEEPING BAG. CUE FALLING
OVER AND GETTING STUCK BETWEEN
SPINDLES FOR HOURS UNTIL SOMEONE
COULD SAVE ME.

I stared at the computer screen, my brows drawn down into a frown. I'd just spent the last hour trying to make sense of this schedule for next week, but I couldn't for the life of me work it out.

Tilting my head, I tried to look at it from another point of view. "This makes no sense." I moved the mouse over the spreadsheet, looking at the dates along the left-side column.

I growled, throwing my good hand up in the air. It was no use, I felt like I was staring at the most complicated mathematical equation known to man. I pushed my chair back and marched toward Axel's office.

It had been over a week since the near kiss and the knee-in-the-balls situation. Axel had barely spoken to me, remaining professional as he gave me rides to work each morning after helping me put on my brace. This morning I managed to work out how to get it on myself, so by the time he turned up at my door, I was ready and waiting for him.

When I told him what I'd done, I couldn't work out

whether he was happy he didn't have to put it on me anymore, or sad. Either way, I totally bossed being an adult. And then this happened—a simple schedule confused the bejeezus out of me.

I knocked once on his door and opened it up. "Axel? I have no idea what this—" I cut myself off when I looked up and saw him on the phone. "Oh, sorry," I whispered.

He shook his head, a small smile on his face as he waved me forward and pointed to the chair opposite his desk.

"I'll be there, Jared." Axel watched me as I took a seat, his gaze burning a path as he followed the curve of my neck. He chuckled. "Yeah, I'll bring a plus one this time." He rolled his eyes at something Jared said. "I'm sure my brother will be there, too. I'll ask him when I see him… Yeah… I'll see you Sunday evening."

He placed the handset down in its cradle and blew out a deep breath, massaging his temples. He ran his palm along the stubble on his jaw, and I willed my eyes not to close so I could relish in the sound of the hair scraping against his hand. What was it about that sound that made butterflies spread from my stomach to my vagina?

My eyes widened, almost as if they were warning me to not say or do something stupid. But how could I possibly hold it all in when he oozed sex from each and every one of his pores?

"I need you to attend a charity event with me in a few weeks."

My head reeled back. I knew this could be a possibility, but since I'd broke my collarbone a couple of weeks ago, I thought he wouldn't want me to go. "You do?"

"I'll make sure you have a dress and heels to wear. Someone can come to your room and do your hair and makeup so you don't strain your…" He tilted his head to my shoulder. "You should be more healed by then anyway."

I raised a brow. "What if I want to go fresh-faced with my frizzy hair untamed?"

"You can go in your pajamas for all I care, as long as you're there to help me bat everyone away."

"What event is it?" I asked, leaning back in the chair, and feeling like I finally had control over my own body again.

"A family friend is raising money for a new children's ward for one of the hospitals in the city." He let out a breath. "I already donate so I don't see why I have to go…" He trailed off, looking out of the windows of his office. "Anyway, what did you want?"

I stood and walked around his desk, clicking on his mouse and showing him the shared file. "I don't understand a word of this."

He gazed over the schedule, made a couple of adjustments and pointed out where I went wrong. His alarm rang out, signaling his next meeting, so I backed away with a smile pulling at my lips.

"Thanks. I don't think spreadsheets are my strong point."

He chuckled. "That's okay, your meeting notes are some of the best I've seen. They're detailed, and you never leave anything out. I prefer that to an immaculate schedule."

"Oh, well, awesome!" I fist-bumped the air. "I knew I was bossing today." I pointed at him as I stepped back, my fluffy socks sliding on the floor a little. "Bossed it like the boss."

"What language are you talking?" His voice was rough and demanding, but the twinkle shining in his eyes and the slight quirk of his lips told me he found me funny. *Of course he did. I'm hilarious.*

"Don't act like you don't understand me, Axel." I wagged my finger at him. "You totally wake up and tell yourself you're gonna be a badass boss."

"Yeah." He stood, pulled his jacket on, and stepped around his desk. "That's exactly what I do. I look in the mirror and ask myself what I see."

"You do?" I asked as I took another step back.

"Yep."

"And what do you see?"

His brows drew down as he said, "I see pride." I burst out laughing at his awful Jamaican accent. "I see power… I see a badass mother who don't take no crap off nobody."

My stomach cramped, and I held my hand against it, wincing slightly but not able to stop it from overtaking my whole body. Tears ran down my face, and I wiped them away as I stood fully.

"You totally *didn't* boss that."

"Hey!" His brows lifted. "I do an awesome Jamaican accent."

"Mmm-hmm." I bit my bottom lip. "You keep telling yourself that."

His cell went off in his hand, but he ignored it. "You do one then."

"Huh?"

"You do an accent."

"Me?" I pointed at my chest and looked around as if

there could have been someone else here he was talking to. "I can't do accents."

"Ohhh, so you can tell me mine isn't good, but you can't even do one?"

"Well… I… I can do a Southern accent?" He waved his hand at me to go on, so I cleared my throat. "Now don't you git sassy with meh, mister. I'll be fixin' to teach you a lesson."

He rolled his lips between his teeth, his cheeks reddening as he held his breath. But he finally lost his battle, and his laughter erupted out of him, brash and deep.

"Hey! That was good."

"You sounded…" He heaved a breath. "You sounded like a Southern grandma."

I gasped, long and loud. "How dare you!" Spinning around to hide the grin on my face, I didn't notice the glass door until it was too late and it was smacking into my forehead. "Ahh, fuck!"

Axel's laughter died off immediately. "Vi?"

"I'm okay," I told him after I'd lifted my hand to my head and checked I wasn't bleeding. My head thumped a little, but I did a Taylor Swift and shook it off. I stepped back and pulled open the door. I raised a brow and turned back to face Axel. "The door attacked me. You should fire it."

He chuckled, shaking his head as he walked out behind me. "I've never seen someone so…"

"Don't say it," I warned, planting my hand on my hip.

"Klutzy."

"That's it, you said it." I huffed.

He winked, spun around, and headed toward the elevators.

"I'm gonna mess up your whole schedule now!" I shouted after him. He waved in that way old ladies do when they think you're acting preposterous and turned the corner.

Why was he so infuriating but sexy at the same time?

———

I tilted my head as I took stock of myself in the mirror, quite proud of the fact that I'd managed to tame my frizzy mane. It normally took hours and way too many products to achieve it, but there was something about the air in New York—probably on account of it being freezing cold.

Stepping back, I trailed my hand down my side and over my hip. The soft material of the khaki maxi dress flowed through my fingers, and the split up the side wafted, showing my legs which were smoother than they'd ever been. I winced as I thought about this afternoon. I didn't want to spend hours shaving, so I found a beauty salon to get them *waxed*. I wanted to say I'd never do it again, but the after effects were *so* worth it.

I switched the bathroom light off and headed into the bedroom where I grabbed my clutch bag and jacket. There was no way in hell I was going to try and get both arms through the thing, so I placed it over my forearm as I exited my room.

I was fifteen minutes early to meet El, and I wanted to surprise her downstairs—and not let her see my messy room. She was a neat freak, and if she spotted the mess, I knew she'd spend the next few hours cleaning up after me.

Yesterday I'd told her I needed to get out of the room, so we were going out for dinner. She jumped on the opportunity of girl time and said she knew the perfect place and to dress nice. So here I was, in a dress and some strappy heels I probably shouldn't take the risk in, but wearing flats wouldn't have the same impact.

I stepped out of the elevator and made my way over to the bar, deciding I'd have a *small* drink while I waited for El to get here.

The bartender passed me my drink, and I leaned my back against the bar, starting to people-watch—my favorite pastime. That was until a loud laugh echoed above everyone else's murmurings.

I turned my head and smiled when I spotted El sitting with a guy on her left, looking at her like she hung the moon. I didn't remember Chad, but I knew he was there after I passed out last week—according to El.

Holding my glass in one hand, I pushed off the bar and stepped toward them, catching the last bit of El's conversation.

"So, you're telling me *you* have been helping a woman you barely know? I can't believe—" Her eyes widened when she saw me, several emotions crossing her features. Shock being the most obvious one. Why was she shocked? "No," she whispered, standing up.

I frowned, tilting my head at her.

Chad stood beside her and moved toward me. "Nice to see you again," he said, his deep voice cutting through the silence.

"You too," I whispered. "Although I don't remember the first time."

He chuckled and moved his attention to the other guy whose back was to me. That's when his face filled with the same shock El's was still stuck in. I pushed my hip out, planting my hand on it. "Why are you both looking like that?" At the sound of my voice, the other guy turned. "What—why are you…"

"Vi," Axel breathed, his lips lifting into a smile as he pushed out of his chair. "What are you…"

"She's my cousin," El blurted out at the same time Chad said, "He's my brother."

My brows lifted, and my head reeled back. The force made me wobble on my feet, and Axel lunged forward, grasping my waist to right me.

"He was just telling us about helping someone who broke their collarbone…" El shook her head. "I should've put it together."

"You know El?" I asked Axel when El turned to face Chad.

"I do. She's my brother's girlfriend."

"Oh." I bit my bottom lip, causing his gaze to flick down to it. I couldn't help thinking about the last time he looked at me in the same way…and what happened afterward. He seemed to be thinking the same thing because he slowly let go and twisted his hips so his junk wasn't in line with my knees.

Good call.

We were all silent for several minutes, each of us looking at each other until Chad broke it by clapping his hands. "Well, we were both going to get dinner separately, but we may as well all go together as Vi and Axel already know each other."

"Her name is Violet," Axel growled and bent down to pick up his drink, downing it in one swallow.

"Whoa." Chad held his hands up, his eyes wide, something in their depths only Axel seemed to be able to decipher. "My bad, I didn't realize—"

"Don't," Axel warned and pulled his cell out, his thumb clicking on the screen.

El finally looked back at me, a secret smile on her face as she rounded the chairs and headed over to me. Her arm wrapped around my shoulder and she pulled me closer, squeezing.

"Ah, shit. Careful, El."

She gasped, letting me go. "Fuck!" I winced and placed my drink on the table, having only had one sip but deciding I needed painkillers more than alcohol right now. "I'm sorry, Vi."

"It's okay," I murmured, trying to open my clutch bag. Pulling out the painkillers prescribed to me, I popped two out into my hand and stowed the bottle away.

"You in pain?" Axel asked, concern flashing in his blue eyes.

"A little." I shuffled. "Do you have any water?"

He nodded and walked away, leaving me, Chad, and El standing like lemons.

"I'm sorry," El repeated.

"Seriously, El. It's okay. It was already hurting from trying to tame this mane." I pointed at my head, chuckling at myself.

She trailed her gaze from my strappy heels all the way up to my hair. "You look…sexy, *hot*, smoking."

I shook my head at the different voices she made. "Shut up."

"You do!" She turned around to Chad. "Tell her she looks hot, Chad!"

"I…" His gaze flicked away. "I don't think—"

"Tell her!" El insisted, moving closer to him. "She's seriously smoking. I mean look at those boobs… Oh, wait!" She threw her head back. "Your brother's already seen them."

"El," I groaned.

"Sorry, Vi." *She didn't sound sorry.* "Tell her, Chad! Tell her she's hot."

He shifted uncomfortably. His gaze didn't meet mine because it was focused on something behind me, his face becoming more taut.

"Leave him alone, El."

She twirled around. "You'll never believe it coming from me, but when it comes from someone else, you will, so Chad needs to tell you you're hot!"

"Don't you dare," a rough voice warned from right behind me. A glass of water was handed to me, and I turned, seeing Axel's face pinched in warning.

"I wasn't gonna," Chad said, grabbing El's hand and pulling her along with him. "We'll see you at the restaurant."

El started to say something, but when Chad whispered in her ear, she winked and happily skipped off with him. *She literally skipped.*

"I see how you managed to get yourself in trouble last week."

I lifted the water to my lips, took the pills, and settled the glass on the table next to my other discarded drink. "Yeah." I chuckled. "She can find trouble anywhere."

"Must run in the family, then," he commented, his lips spreading into a grin as his cell beeped in his pocket. "Our ride is here."

"Our ride?" I asked, following him out of the bar and past Al, who was standing at the main doors. "Hey, Al."

"Miss Scott." He nodded. "Looking lovely tonight. Enjoy your date."

"Oh, no." I waved him off. "This isn't a—"

"Thanks, Al," Axel interrupted, placing his hand on my back and propelling me through the doors.

I growled, earning me laughter. "You don't play fair. You broke your own rule."

"I did?"

"Yeah, you interrupted me."

He shrugged but didn't reply. I wanted to stomp my foot like a child, but instead, I harrumphed and walked past him to the car Jeeves was waiting in at the sidewalk. "Ohhh, you can be such an assh—"

"Don't finish that sentence." His chest pressed against my back as I pulled the door open. Neither of us moved as his breath skirted over my neck and elicited goose bumps. *Traitorous body.* Axel skimmed his long fingers across my waist and squeezed the flesh over my lower ribs. I shivered when he tucked his face into the crook of my neck and ran his nose along the soft skin. "You smell so good." He lifted his lips to my ear and whispered, "They're right. You look beautiful tonight."

I held back the moan wanting to slip free and turned my head, not believing what he had said. Our gazes clashed, but all I witnessed was the truth shining back at me. I didn't know what to say or what to do, so I replied, "Thanks, you too," and pulled away from him, pushing into the back of the car.

I missed the heat of his body against mine, but I knew if I didn't get away from him right now, I would do something I regretted—like injuring him again.

The soft, cool leather seats cooled my hot skin, and I closed my eyes, trying to gather my thoughts. And that's when I realized what I said. *Thanks, you too?*

Jeez.

———

"This one time we were out riding our bikes around the neighborhood, and we saw this hill, so we made our way up it. 'I'm gonna go down and try to fly,' she says to me. Now, me being me, and knowing Vi, I *know* she's gonna get hurt, so I try to tell her, but she pulls her shoulders back, giving me a determined look before she pushes off the top of the hill." El laughed so loud the whole restaurant turned to look at her. She didn't care though as she continued on with her fifth story of the night. "I'm at the top, watching her go down, and then all of a sudden, she shouts—"

"My brakes aren't working," I cut in.

I decided after the third story I may as well join in with telling them. When you look back at them, they were funny. I mean, we all had those moments as kids where we were so clumsy we thought we wouldn't get through the whole day. It normally stopped when we hit adulthood. *Normally.*

"Noooo." Chad leaned forward, his attention focused on El, enthralled in each and every story she told. "Then what happened?"

"She flies down this hill, her front wheel getting stuck in a rabbit hole." El lifted her arms in the air. "Then, *boom*! She goes over the handlebars, does some weird twisty shit in the air and lands on her back."

"Ouch." Axel winced.

I grimaced at him. "Yeah. I dislocated my shoulder."

El nodded knowingly as she lifted her spoonful of cheesecake to her lips and snorted. "Do you remember the summer trip after high school?"

"No, El." I groaned. "Not that one, please—"

"We went to Mexico for the week, right? So, we're in the sea…" El's eyes twinkled. "Then, all of a sudden, I hear, 'Everyone out of the sea! There's something in there! Shark! Shark!' People start rushing out of the sea along with Vi. When she makes it out of the water, screaming that she's been bitten, I look down at her leg, and there's a crab attached to her."

I snorted with laughter. Now that one I was embarrassed about for weeks because I was—

"She was known as 'crab girl' for the whole week."

I closed my eyes, the smile on my face unable to be wiped away. However much she retold these stories didn't matter because I was spending time with her. El must have sensed my thoughts because when I opened my eyes, she was staring at me with a sad look on her face. "I'm going to miss you when you're gone."

"Me too," I whispered, reaching over and squeezing her hand.

"When do you leave?" Chad asked.

"Day after Christmas."

"You should come to our parents' for Christmas Day so you can spend some time together. They'd love to meet some of El's family, too."

"Oh, no." I waved my hand. "I wouldn't want to intrude—"

"You should come," Axel said from next to me. His blue eyes were shadowed with something I couldn't decipher.

"I should?" I asked.

Everything seemed to fade away as he stared at me. I jumped a little in my seat when his long fingers gripped my knee over the material of my dress. My breath caught in my throat as his thumb rubbed back and forth, grazing the soft skin peeking through the slit of the dress.

"Yeah." His voice was lower this time. "You should."

I wanted to tell him my normal Christmas Day was spent sitting in front of the TV watching Christmas movies while eating my weight in chips and candy. I hadn't had a proper Christmas since I left home at eighteen.

"I...okay."

His lips lifted into a smile, the same one that made butterflies dance in my stomach and my skin go hot. I let out a long breath and smiled back.

Damn, a woman would kill to have that smile directed at her.

Chapter 7

CONFESSION #3: I WENT OUT WITH ODD SHOES ON... YEAH, IT WAS AN AWESOME DAY.

"I've never been on a boat."

Axel kept walking beside me and tilted his head but didn't look at me directly. He was too busy typing away on his cell as we moved toward the boat. No, boat was too small of a word. It was a yacht, one of those huge ones, probably complete with fancy gadgets.

I'd lived in LA all of my life, and yet I'd never been out on the water. I was dangerous enough on dry land. I hadn't wanted to find out what I was like when I wasn't.

It had been four weeks since the meeting with Mr. Johnson, and both Axel and I had gone back and forth with him and his PA. Now we were invited to join him out on the water.

Yay.

Not.

Axel had had the biggest grin on his face since we found out yesterday, and it was addictive. The whole office had been in a good mood, and I had no doubt it was because of the potential prospects this meeting could present.

"You'll be fine—" Axel turned to face me fully, and halted. His dark-blue eyes widened, and his lips twisted. I could tell he was thinking about all the times I'd fallen over. "It'll be okay. Just…try not to be so…" He waved his hand at me.

I raised a brow and tilted my head, waiting for him to complete his sentence. He didn't. Instead, he looked around, probably trying to distinguish which huge yacht was Mr. Johnson's. I flicked my gaze left and right, spotting someone waving at us, so I lifted my arm.

"Over there," I told Axel and stepped forward onto the wooden slats that made up the small walkway to all of the boats.

Goose bumps trailed over my skin from how close Axel was following me. I wasn't imagining the tension that flowed between us, right? Or maybe I was. Maybe I was in my own little world where all the looks he gave me meant something, and every little touch was because he couldn't stop himself.

Yep. That was totally it.

I chuckled at myself, but as I did, the toe of my stupid new boat shoes got caught in between one of the slats. Axel's hands landed on my waist to right me, the warmth seeping through the material of my tank top and causing my breath to stall in my chest. I looked down, seeing his fingers flex against my ribs. How could hands look so freaking good? It should be illegal to have arms and hands like his. Damn him!

"Not that I'm keeping count or anything, but that's the third time you've nearly tripped in the last hour."

My face heated to epic proportions. I had no clue if it was embarrassment or the fact that his body heat was warming my back and I just wanted to take one little step back so I could relish in it even more.

His hands were gone all too soon though, and then he was standing next to me. I glanced up and pushed some hair behind my ear, cleared my throat, and straightened as I tried to style it out.

"Well, if you hadn't made me get these stupid boat shoes, then maybe I wouldn't resemble Bambi right now. Who the hell has shoes only to wear on boats?" I shook my head. "People are insane."

"Yeah." He scoffed. "It's the shoes."

He started to move toward the boat, and I gritted my teeth. "Hey!" I followed him, making sure I was extra careful not to catch these stupid shoes. When it happened again, I halted and pulled them off my feet. "You can be so...so...mean."

He chuckled, and I couldn't stop the smile from lifting my lips.

Could he just *stop*?

Stop being so sexy. Stop being so nice. Just...*stop*.

"Mr. Taylor, Miss Scott."

I nearly slammed into Axel's back where he'd stopped in front of the yacht, but I saved myself. *See? I wasn't that bad.*

"You must be Miss Jenna," Axel said.

"I certainly am." I peeked around Axel and was greeted by a woman with white hair, and not the fashionable kind that I could never pull off in a million years, but the old woman kind. I tried to cover my shock, but I wasn't sure I managed it. I hadn't expected Mr. Johnson's PA to be so...well... Old.

"Mr. Johnson is waiting for you on top." She waved her arm toward herself and spun around. "Follow me."

Axel stepped back and tilted his head at me to go first. I gripped onto the metal bar, placed my foot on the first step, climbed the next four, and made it onto the boat.

Holy flaming cheese monkeys! It was insane. The wooden decking was polished to within an inch of its life, and the more I moved, the more in awe I became.

A set of six loungers sat off to the left with what looked like a bed in front of it, covered in red and blue pillows. But what really had my mouth hanging open was the jacuzzi in front of that. Who had a jacuzzi on their yacht? Well, this dude did. *Dayum*.

I could hear Axel's footsteps behind me as we moved up to the next level and past that to the top where Mr. Johnson was standing next to all the controls.

"Miss Scott, so nice to see you again."

I swallowed. "You too." I placed my hand in his outstretched one and shook it. "This is freaking amazing."

He chuckled and let go of my hand, moving onto Axel. I didn't hear any of what they said because a guy was handing me a drink and leading me to one of the huge leather seats.

I sat and swiveled on the chair—it actually swiveled—and looked around at the city in front of us. Who knew Manhattan could be so beautiful? I was in awe of every little thing, and I had no doubt I looked like a little girl at her first fun fair, engrossed in all the lights and rides, but I didn't care.

Mr. Johnson started the engine, and I shuffled forward on the seat, watching as the water parted for the front of the boat. Did those things have a proper name? I was aware that there was all this boat lingo like starboard…starborn? I had no idea what it was called. I should have looked it up before I came on here. Crap.

Once we were away from the dock, Mr. Johnson handed the reins over to the guy who had passed me my drink.

"Shall we head down and have a chat?" he asked.

I looked up and spotted Axel watching me with a smile on his face. He shook it off and stepped forward. "Sure."

I sighed. I was going to miss all of the beautifulness by having to go inside.

"Why don't you go and relax for a while?"

I pointed at my chest and raised my brows at Axel. "Me?"

He took two steps toward me and crouched down. "Yeah. You've been working hard these last few weeks." He lowered his voice. "If it weren't for you, we wouldn't be having this meeting right now, so just relax for a while."

He didn't have to tell me twice.

I stood and dropped my boat shoes in front of the chair, causing Axel to stumble as he tried to stand himself. I couldn't stop the snort at watching his arms windmill. "Looks like it's not just me who's clumsy, huh?" I patted him on the shoulder and walked past him, back the way we came and down to the loungers.

No one had followed me down, but I was okay with that. Since coming to New York, I hadn't just chilled out, not even to binge watch. I didn't mind the workload, but a girl needed to relax every now and again.

I could imagine me pulling off my tank top and shorts, and lowering myself to the lounger, letting the sun rays beat down on my skin. There was only one problem with that though, it was freaking winter.

Trust it to be just my luck that I get to be on a ridiculously awesome yacht in winter instead of the summer. But that wasn't going to deter me. Nope. I was going to lie here and pretend it was June and not December.

And that was exactly what I did, and okay, maybe I had a nap too, but who wouldn't? Naps were the best invention ever. You had to be careful with them though. If you slept for too long, then you'd feel like poop afterward, not enough and the same thing. But I'd got mine down to a fine art. At least, I thought I had, because this time instead of being woken up by my cell vibrating, I was being covered with something.

My eyes sprang open, and I was greeted with the darkening sky and Axel's face. "Axel?" I asked, my voice groggy.

"Yeah?"

"How long have I been asleep?"

He shrugged and quirked his lips on one side. "Only a few hours."

"Well...shit." I sat up, scrubbed my hand down my face, and looked around. I couldn't see Mr. Johnson or Miss Jenna anywhere. "How did the meeting go?"

His quirked lips turned into a full-on grin as he leaned toward me. "He's getting his lawyers to contact ours."

"No way!"

"Yes way." He chuckled and placed his hands on either side of my legs. "I talked him through all of the plans, and he's all for it. He said there may even be some other companies he can send my way too."

I lifted my hand and placed it on his cheek, my grin

taking over my whole face. "That's amazing, Axel. This is it, the break you wanted."

"It is." He nodded and pushed his face into my hand, his gaze not moving off my eyes.

The lights from the buildings twinkled against his dark-blue irises, and I couldn't look away, not even if I wanted to. I could sense that he wanted to move forward, and I licked my lips in preparation. They tingled, almost as if he'd already placed his against mine.

His gaze flicked down to my lips, and I waited for him to make the first move. Surely this would be it now? He'd finally kiss me, and fireworks would go off around us, just like in the movies.

"Vi," he whispered.

My hand fell away from his face, and I moved closer. We were only centimeters apart now, and the tension was insane. Then the yacht halted, and the momentum had us clashing heads and completely ruining the moment.

I winced and pulled away. "Ow."

Axel stood, looking anywhere but me as he murmured, "We better head off," and handed me the white boat shoes.

"Right." I stared up at him, wondering if he was going to say or do something else, but when he didn't, I lifted off the sun lounger and pushed my feet inside the shoes.

Mr. Johnson and Miss Jenna came down from the top, and we said our goodbyes, exited the boat, and walked back toward the waiting car.

"I can't believe I slept through all of that." I huffed

out a breath and pulled the car door open, but Axel's hand covered mine to stop me from slipping inside.

"I'll bring you back out on the water."

I turned my head. "You will?"

"I will. I have a yacht too."

My eyes widened, and my mouth hung open. "You do?"

"Yep, but maybe I'll bring you out in the summer instead so you don't..." His gaze flicked down to my chest and back up again. "Get too cold."

When I looked down, my nipples were pointing right at him. What a perfect way to end the day.

———

"As you can see, there's no other option but to split the company apart. I'm in negotiations right now, and I should have the deal closed before we go on Christmas break in a few weeks."

My finger slid over the tablet screen. I wasn't taking in any of the information Axel was saying. After I started this position, I soon realized that I needed to record the meetings to catch everything that was said. I tended to get bored after about ten minutes, and this meeting had now just hit sixty, so I was *mega* bored—or I would be if I weren't sitting at the back of the room with an earbud in one of my ears and a new Netflix series playing on the tablet, and they were none the wiser.

Looking up, I saw Axel in the midst of a speech. I checked that my cell was still recording him and pushed the other earbud in.

The starting sequence to American Vandal played. I was two episodes in, and I *had* to know who drew the dicks. There was no way it was Dylan—it was plain as day because he drew hairs on the balls and the heads were completely different.

I was engrossed, my mind working overtime as I watched them start to make a timeline of events.

Leaning back, I let the next episode play automatically.

"What the!" I jumped off my chair, the tablet nearly falling to the floor, but Axel's hand came out to catch it. As he did, the earbuds were yanked out of my ears. "Ow!"

"What are you doing?" He was using his office voice, the one that made me shiver.

"I…" I looked around the room, seeing it empty. How long was I watching? "Erm…research?"

He raised a brow, lifting the tablet and glancing down at where it was paused—right on an image of a dick sketch. "On how to draw dicks? Is this your obsession, Vi?"

A blush spread over my chest and up my cheeks. "Erm…" I needed to style this out. "Well, I mean…it's important."

"It is?" He placed the tablet down on the table, widened his stance, and crossed his arms over his chest.

I nodded. "It is. So, this show, they're trying to work out who drew the dicks."

"Who drew the dicks?"

I pointed at him. "Exactly! I need to know. I don't think it's Dylan. I mean, sure, he draws them everywhere else, but—"

"Dylan?"

"The guy they suspended! They didn't even have

enough evidence." I'm outraged. They didn't even consider the fact it may be someone else.

Axel's lips quirked. Didn't he get this was serious? "So, these dicks? How do you know it's not...Dylan?"

I looked around the room, my teeth sinking into my bottom lip. I spotted the whiteboard on the far wall and headed toward it. "I'll show you."

He didn't say anything as he followed me around the large table, leaned against it, and watched me. His shirt sleeves were rolled up to his elbows again, and it took great inner strength not to keep focused on them.

Wait...what was I doing? *Dicks.*

I twirled to face the board and picked up a black pen. "So, these are the dicks Dylan draws around the school." I pressed the tip of the pen on the board and filled up half of it with the same kind of dick. I placed some hairs on the balls, making sure the head was the same as *he'd* draw. "Now." I turned my head and met Axel's gaze. "The dicks drawn on the teachers' cars looked like this." I faced the board again, drew the same kind of dick, placed the lid on the pen and stepped to the side.

"Okay..."

"Can you see the difference? The heads? The ball hairs?"

He choked on a laugh. "Ball hairs?"

"Uh-huh."

He tilted his head to the side, studying them intently. "I never thought I'd be studying dicks today."

I waited for nearly a minute and asked, "Can you see it?"

He stood and moved a step closer to me. "Yeah, I can."

"See! Dylan didn't do it!" I raised my arm out to the side and slapped my thigh.

Axel arched a brow. "He may not have, but why are you watching that while you should be working?"

I swallowed. "Erm… I was bored?"

His lips flattened into a straight line and there was something shining in his eyes that I couldn't quite place. "Whether you're bored or not, you should be paying attention."

I walked around him and collected my cell, which was still recording. "It's okay, I record all your meetings."

He stared at me like I had two giant heads. "That's actually a good idea." He grinned.

"I know." I smirked, placed the cell down on the table next to the tablet, and grabbed the small block to rub the dicks off the whiteboard. "I'm a genius."

"Well… I wouldn't go that far."

I gasped, my hand flying to my chest. "You wound me." I pulled a face like I was dying and laughed.

"You're one of a kind, Vi." His deep laugh echoed around us, and I wanted to bathe in it, strip it from him, and listen to it over and over again.

I wiped the block on the board, scrubbing harder when it didn't seem to budge. I frowned, wondering what I was doing wrong. Picking the pen up off the little ledge, my eyes widened. *Shit!*

"Erm… Axel?"

"Yeah?" came his gruff reply from a couple of feet behind me. "What would you say if I told you I accidentally drew these dicks with a Sharpie?"

"I'd say you better be joking."

I stared at the two giant dicks in horror. He had a

meeting in this room in ten minutes, and these dicks were not moving in the slightest.

"I..."

"Tell me you didn't, Vi."

I cleared my throat, forced a smile onto my face and turned to face him. "I didn't."

His body relaxed as he pulled a chair out and was about to sit down.

"But I did." I looked anywhere but at him. The chairs, the pitcher sitting in the middle of the table filled with water, out of the windows at the stupid skyline that I hated but simultaneously loved.

He stepped over to me, grabbed the block out of my hand, and scrubbed the board over and over again, but it still wouldn't budge. "Fuck!" He slammed the palm of his hand against the board. "Shit. Fuck!"

"It's okay!" I rushed forward, picking up the Sharpie. "I can disguise it."

I put the tip to the...tip of the penis. Drawing lines and wiggles, not stopping until I thought they were unrecognizable.

Stepping back, I continued to the back of the room, taking a good long look. Axel stared at it. "Now it looks like a pussy and two dicks. They're double teaming her!" he thundered.

Crapola. He was right. I'd just made a bad drawing even worse. Maybe I should black the whole board out? That way no one—

"Mr. Taylor? Your next client is here," Freya, who ran the front desk, announced.

My eyes widened to epic proportions, so much so that I was sure my eyeballs were going to pop out of my head any second. We both stared at each other as three guys were led into the room, their gazes landing on the board.

"I'll just erm…" I hooked my thumb over my shoulder, sliding across the floor in my fluffy socks. Since the first day I wore them, Axel hadn't said a thing about them, so I took it as permission to wear them all the time. It was his fault, anyway, for wanting his office to resemble a freezer.

"Oh, no, you don't." He grabbed my right arm, pulled me beside him, pasted on a smile, and held his hand out to the guys in front of him.

They all exchanged pleasantries until the youngest one—considering the other two were at least sixty, it wasn't saying much—said, "Hey, that looks like one of them American Vandal dicks."

I gasped. "Have you watched it?"

"Yeah." He nodded as he sat down. "Funny as shit."

I pulled out the chair opposite him, my eyes not leaving his. "It wasn't Dylan, right? Wait!" I held my palm up. "Don't tell me. You'll spoil it."

He laughed, leaning back in his seat. "Taylor, you didn't tell me your new PA was—"

"Don't finish that sentence, Jared," Axel warned.

I frowned, sure I'd heard the name before.

"She's your plus one?"

Axel turned to face me, a brow raised. "If she survives that long."

"Ouch. You gonna fire her?"

Axel watched me for a beat. "Nah. She's entertaining. I think I'll keep her."

I swallowed, wanting to shoot some kind of comeback. But my vagina was screaming, *"Keep me, too!"*

Chapter 8

CONFESSION #67: I WALKED AROUND
THE PARK WITH MY SKIRT STUCK IN MY
PANTIES... COVERED IN HUGE SMILEY
FACES.

I placed the champagne flute on a table and snatched another one from a server's tray. I couldn't remember how many drinks I'd had, but I had a nice buzz going on.

I'd been on my own for the last hour while Axel talked to some new business partners or something or other. I had no idea who they were exactly, just that they could be important.

I didn't expect to be abandoned as soon as we got here. Especially not after I'd spent the whole day having my hair and makeup done, and definitely not while I was wearing my trusty little black dress. Thank God I'd been able to not wear my sling and only my brace underneath.

I knew a total of one person, and he was currently talking to a woman with legs as long as the stupid skyscrapers in this city. *Ugh.*

Downing this glass, I then plucked another one off a tray and maneuvered through the crowd and over to Axel. Her hand was pressed against his chest. Any other person wouldn't see how uncomfortable he was, but I saw the way his eyes crinkled at the corners and the way he tried to step back from her when she leaned toward him. She followed. *Of course the crackwhore followed.*

Maybe I'd had one too many drinks because the jealous monster was coming forth and there was nothing I could do to stop her.

I stepped beside Axel, looking crackwhore right in the eyes. I turned to face him, resting my hand on his bicep and cooed, "Hey, baby," way too loudly. He frowned down at me with questions in his eyes. Lifting up onto my tiptoes, I whispered, "Go with it if you want to get rid of her."

He turned his head, his lips centimeters from mine, as his eyes flashed. "Hey." His arm slid around my waist as he pulled me closer. My glass toppled between us, but neither of us looked away. "Where have you been?"

"I…" I flicked my gaze over to crackwhore, seeing the sneer on her face. *Yeah, bitch, you wish you were in these arms.* "I had to freshen up." I bit my bottom lip. "I forgot to wear panties."

Why. The. Hell. Did. I. Just. Say. That?

His hand trailed down my back and stopped on my ass where he splayed his warm palm.

"Well, I guess I'll go and…" I blocked out crackwhore, basking in the feel of him. I heard her footsteps as she walked away, but Axel didn't let go.

"You're playing with fire."

"I'm a pyromaniac."

His breath quickened, and he yanked me closer as his fingertips dug into my ass. "Careful, Vi. If I didn't know any better, I'd say you wanted me."

Leaning my head back, I looked up at him as I lifted onto my tiptoes. "Who said I didn't?"

Great. Now horny Vi had made an appearance.

We both stared at each other, promises being made that shouldn't be considered. But would it really be so bad? I'd be back in LA soon, and he'd be here. We wouldn't see each other again, so one night of him ripping my clothes off couldn't hurt, right?

He ducked his head, took a deep breath, and ran his nose along my neck and up to my ear where he whispered, "You have one chance to tell me you don't want this. Say it now, because if you don't, I won't be able to hold myself back."

I moaned as he trailed kisses along the soft skin under my ear. "I want this. I want you and your arm veins."

"My arm veins?" he asked, chuckling but still planting soft kisses along the side of my neck. *Could you die from kisses?*

"Mmm-hmm." I traced my fingers along his arm, though I couldn't see them through his jacket. "I want them." He pulled back, his dark-blue eyes nearly black as I continued, "I want you."

I looked around the room, wondering if we could leave right now.

Axel's nostrils flared when I stepped back and out of his arms. I gave him a coy smile, sunk my teeth into my bottom lip, and sauntered back another step, loving the sexy vibe I was giving off. That was until my foot wobbled. My eyes widened as I imagined a repeat of the bar happening, but I didn't fall this time. Instead, I was pulled into a pair of strong arms.

"You're a danger to yourself."

I laughed. "I know. But you wanna have sex with this danger."

He chuckled along with me, shaking his head. "What will I do with you?"

I glanced up at him and placed my drink on the table I nearly tripped over. "I can think of many things you can do." I waggled my brows up and down. "They involve my lady garden and your member."

He choked out a sound I'd never heard before. "Don't ever refer to them as that again." He pulled back, taking my hand and leading me out of the room.

"Channel and rod?" I asked.

His head reeled back as we collected our coats. "Definitely not."

"How about meat flaps and—"

The man standing at the door stared at me like I'd just escaped from a mental hospital as Axel placed his hand over my mouth, muffling me. "That's enough of that. If you want my dick in your pussy, then you'll stop referring to them in that manner." He raised his brows, asking silently if I was going to stop. When I nodded, he let go and led me toward the waiting car.

"It's okay," I started. "I know you want to put your money in my coin purse."

He groaned, opening the door. "Get your ass in this car otherwise my disco stick won't be doing any dancing."

I stared at him, my mouth hanging open in shock. "You did *not* just call your dick a disco stick."

He grinned. "I did. And it felt really good."

All the bravado I felt at the charity event slowly faded away as we got closer to the hotel. The atmosphere was intense in the back of the car, the air fizzling and crackling around us.

Axel exited the car when we pulled up and held his hand for me to take. I pulled in a breath, putting my small hand in his large one and stepping out of the car. Neither of us said anything as we made our way to the elevators and stepped inside. Axel pushed the key in the small hole next to the P button to take us up to the top floor.

Leaning back against the mirrored wall, I stared at him as his eyes burned with need. They trailed over my body, and he stepped forward causing my breath to stall in my chest. No part of him was touching me and yet my skin was on fire and I was panting like I was about to erupt from his presence.

"Vi." His voice was like a plea to my soul, my body hearing it loud and clear. "This is your last chance. When those doors open, nothing will stop me from taking you the way I wanted to when you first turned up at my office."

"You..." My voice cracked, so I cleared it and tried again. "You wanted me then?"

He tilted his head, gauging my reaction, and when the doors slid open, I pushed off the wall and closed the distance between us. I let my fingers float over his arm as I quirked my lips. "What are you waiting for then?" I asked, my voice like liquid honey. I gave myself a mental high five at the confident tone because I was totally working this seduction right now. Tomorrow I might—most definitely—cringe at myself, but right now, I wanted him with every inch of my body.

I flicked my gaze between his eyes, dropped it to his lips, and brought it back to his flaring eyes. I winked and twirled on my heels, breezing past him out of the elevator and into the penthouse. I was about to turn to look around and take it all in, but his arm wrapped around my waist from behind and my eyes fluttered closed.

He growled in my ear, the sound such a turn-on that I let my head fall back against his shoulder. He grasped the hem of my dress and tugged it up to my waist, exposing me. His hand ran over my hip, causing a moan to escape from my lips.

"You really aren't wearing panties."

I gripped his forearm when his finger slid through me and rubbed my clit in the most delicious way. My eyes widened. What if he didn't like the way I groomed myself?

There were so many different ways to present yourself. How was a girl to know which one men prefer?

Did they like it completely bare? I hated feeling like I never went through puberty.

Did they like a landing strip? A signal to say: *Here! I'm here! Put your airplane—dick—right here.*

Or did they want a giant bush? No, they wouldn't want to have to battle through the pubes to find the clit, right?

His finger entered me and brought me out of my head. I opened my eyes and observed our reflection in the window in front of us.

"You like that?" he asked and trailed his tongue over my neck then blew on it.

"Y-eah," I stammered. "Yeah, I do."

He added another finger and murmured, "So wet. All for me."

I thrust my hips, riding his hand like a seasoned pro, but he was pulling away all too soon.

"What—" I turned around.

He took his jacket off and threw it on the floor. His attention didn't move away from me as he undid each button on his shirt, slowly revealing his tan chest. A smattering of hair on his pecs had me salivating even more than I already was.

His eyes flashed as I staggered forward, planted my hand on his chest, and relished in the velvety skin covering his tensed muscles. He jerked his shirt off, and I couldn't resist trailing my palms over his defined shoulders and down to his forearms.

"These drive me crazy," I told him as I ran the pads of my fingers over his arm veins.

Our gazes locked. There was a beat. Then two. Then three.

And then he was lifting me up off the floor to bring me flush against him. His fingers bit into my ass as he boosted me higher, and I wrapped my legs around his waist.

I moaned as his hard, pants-covered dick rubbed against my inner thigh. "Yesss."

Everything was a blur as he carried me through the apartment and into another room. He placed me on the edge of the bed and grasped the bottom of my dress which was still hiked up around my waist. He pulled, but it became difficult when I couldn't quite raise my left arm.

He struggled for a few seconds and murmured something under his breath, but I couldn't see him, because the dress was covering my face.

"Let me." I tried to stand, squealing when my forehead smacked against something.

"Fuck," he spluttered.

"Shit!" I squeaked, standing with my dress still covering my face. "What just happened?"

"You head-butted me in the nose." He groaned, but not the sexual kind, more of the *I'm in pain*, kind.

I finally managed to get the dress over my head, my wide eyes meeting his where he was standing a few feet away, holding his nose.

"I… I'm sorry." My voice was small, and I started to feel like maybe we shouldn't do this. He was right: I was a danger. I couldn't even have sex without trying to knock the other willing party out.

Axel shook his head, stepped forward, and ripped the dress out of my hands. He grasped my waist and pulled me closer to him. I peeked up as he glanced down, the intense atmosphere swirling around us as he lowered his head, his lips coming closer to mine.

I was naked in front of him, and I realized we hadn't even kissed yet. How the hell had that happened?

His lips met mine, fast, urgent, needing. I grasped onto his biceps as he leaned forward and pushed me onto the bed. He followed, resting his forearms above my head and blocking me in. Not that I wanted to go anywhere, anyway.

He slid his tongue across my lips, demanding me to open up. Who was I to deny my boss?

Moaning when his tongue stroked against mine, I rocked my hips, needing his touch. But he didn't give it to me. Instead, he let go of my mouth and trailed his lips down my body until he was kneeling at the side of the bed in front of me. His hard palms glided along my inner thighs, and he nudged them apart. He lowered his head to my pussy, his dark-blue gaze locked on mine.

"I erm… I…" I bit down on my bottom lip as his hot breath fanned over the sensitive area. "I don't know what you like, but I hate being bare and—"

"Vi—"

"I don't want to feel like I didn't go through puberty. That's just weird, but I don't want a giant bush escaping every time I take my panties off—"

"Violet—"

"If you don't like my land of dinosaurs, then I can—"

One slow lick and I was snapping my mouth shut, practically vibrating with need. He flicked his warm, wet tongue over my clit and I thrust my hips closer to his mouth. I weaved my fingers through his soft hair, but he pulled back all too soon, licking his lips.

He stood, shucked off his pants and lowered his body back over mine. I swallowed as he reached out and retrieved a foil packet, hypnotized as he held it up between us, and ripped it open with his teeth.

Sheathing the condom over his thick shaft, he groaned when the head of his dick pressed against my wetness.

"Give it to me," I begged, feeling like I was going out of my mind.

"How badly do you want it?" he asked, raising a brow, a smirk on his lips.

"As bad as I want chocolate when Aunt Flow is in town."

His head reeled back. "I don't think now is the time to be talking about your aunt."

I snorted, shaking my head as I gripped his shoulders and pushed my hips toward him. "My period, you fruitcake."

His eyes widened as understanding flashed over his face. He was stock-still for a split second, and then he was throwing his head back laughing, every muscle in his body shaking with the force. He looked so sexy when he was open like this, and all it made me want to do was stroke him like he was a new pair of fluffy socks.

Once he gained control of himself, he scrubbed his hand down his face. "I knew sex with you wouldn't be normal."

"Did you expect anything less?" I asked and threw my hand up in the air. "Would you just fuck me already? Jeez, you like to take your time." I rolled my eyes, grinning up at him.

"Maybe I want to make you wait?"

Raising a brow, I tilted my head to the side. "I can always head downstairs and grab Lucas."

"Lucas?" His brows furrowed, a warning shining in the depths of his eyes.

"Yep," I answered, popping the *P*. "My vibrator. I named him after Lucas from *One Tree Hill*."

He chuckled under his breath, pulled back, and drove his hips forward, entering me in one swift move. "Jesus Fucking Christ!"

I held on to him tightly, scared if I let go I'd float away like a feather escaping from a pillow.

His thrusts became erratic, his rhythm completely off as he let himself go. I followed him right into whatever place he'd taken himself to, not feeling anything but his dick and his hands as they grabbed my boobs, squeezing, and rubbing the rough pad of his thumbs over my nipples.

"Yes, right there, Axel. Right. There." The slow burn started at the bottom of my stomach, signaling I was close...*so close*. "Don't stop..." My back bowed as his hand came back to my clit and stroked, bringing me even closer. "Yes! Yes, yes, yes!"

"That's it, Vi. Lose yourself to me...come—"

I opened my eyes, connecting them with his. "Don't say it," I warned, knowing from the look in his eyes what he was about to say. "Don't try and make me come on command. That doesn't ever work."

"You sure about that?" His lips quirked with arrogance as he continued to fuck me, his long fingers stroking against my clit so fast that I was sure he could make actual fire with the force and speed.

"Damn sure," I told him, ending it on a moan when I felt the sparks start to ignite.

"Come for me, Vi."

I cringed, pouting and shaking my head at the laughter shining in his eyes. "Why? Why did you say it? Now my lady garden isn't going to get watered!"

He shrugged, still pushing his dick in and out to his own rhythm. "Always wanted to say it and thought you were the perfect person to say it to."

I lifted my hand, pointed at him, and jabbed my finger in his chest. "I'm not...now make me feel like I'm partying with unicorns."

He stopped all his ministrations for a brief second, and something flashed in his eyes. I bit down on my bottom lip, feeling the burn low in my stomach as he moved again. This time was different. He was faster, more methodical as he held me tighter.

The sparks started again, and I knew he was feeling it too when he slammed his lips against mine and groaned.

I lost myself to the kiss and the way his tongue stroked against mine.

The sparks ignited, lighting the fire inside me.

My toes curled. My hands gripped onto him like he was a life raft in the middle of the ocean.

"Fuck, yes!" I tangled my fingers in his hair and thrust my hips up to his to eek my climax out even more.

My eyes rolled into the back of my head when I felt him pulsing inside me, and he growled in approval.

I totally just bossed my boss.

Chapter 9

CONFESSION #19: I BROKE MY FOOT STANDING STILL.

So, it turned out having sex with your boss made your work day easier. Who knew?

In the three days that followed us having sex, we did it a total of eleven and a half times. The half was when we nearly got caught in the bathroom. If dick is entered but neither got off then it was definitely considered a half, right?

I didn't allow my thoughts to come to the front of my mind as they screamed that it would only be six days before I was heading back to my boring life in LA where I'd only receive orgasms from Lucas again. Nope, I didn't listen to those thoughts one bit.

Who was I kidding? It was all I freaking thought about! Especially now as I stared from my desk into his office, my chin resting on my hand and my gaze tracking the line of his jaw and his lips that had been on every part of my body.

I jumped out of my skin when the phone on my desk rang. I tore my gaze away from Axel and all his godlike sexiness and picked up the handset.

"Hello, Mr. Taylor's office. Violet Scott speaking."

"Hello there, Violet. I was wondering if you could help me? I'm calling from one of the companies Taylor Industries owns—Shards and Co. We're having trouble trying to work out which department we need to contact so have been put through to you."

I straightened in my seat and moved the mouse to the side to bring the computer screen to life.

"Of course I can try to help. What's the problem you're having?"

"None of our phone lines are working and—"

"Wait," I interrupted. "How are you calling me then?"

"Cell?"

I smacked myself on the forehead. "Of course, sorry, carry on."

She went on to tell me everything she and her small team had tried, but I had no idea what to suggest for them to do.

"I think I'm going to put you through to our communications department."

"Please don't put me on hold again."

"I…" I turned my head to look at Axel. He was still busy on his conference call. "Maybe I can give you their number?"

"That would be great," she responded. I reeled off the number to her, said goodbye, and placed the phone back into its cradle.

I glanced at Axel and was about to lean back against the chair when the phone rang again. I didn't check who the caller was as I pulled it off its cradle, my gaze still connected to Axel's biceps.

"Hello, Mr—"

"Violet." I jumped at the sound of Della's—the LA CFO—voice, a squeak escaping my throat.

"Della... I..." I spun the chair around so I wasn't facing Axel, the phone cord curling around me as I did. "How..." I cleared my throat. "What can I do for you?"

There was a click on her end and then she said, "I wanted to see how you were getting on and to make sure you'd be back here next Wednesday after Christmas break."

I twirled around in the chair, faced Axel's office and spotted him at his desk, his gaze trained on me. My eyes widened, almost as if Della could see me through the phone, so I whirled around again, looking away from him.

"Yeah, I'll be back." I paused, waiting to see what she said, but when she was silent, I asked, "Was there anything—"

"When you come back, I need to see you in my office. We need to talk."

Talk? "Talk? Can I ask what about?" I moved my feet to spin back around to face Axel's office again, only this time he wasn't in there.

I continued to turn, searching for him. Where had he disappeared to? He was my eye candy, and now it was taken away from me. I was half a revolution away from facing the office again when the phone wire completely wrapped around me. I yanked, trying to undo myself but all it caused was the handset to crash to the floor with a reverberating bang.

"Ahhh." The phone fell out of my hand, tangling with the wire as I batted at it. "I'm stuck! It's tightening. Get it off! Get it—"

Axel's head dipped close to mine from out of

nowhere, causing my heartbeat to speed up and my nerves to rattle.

He picked up the phone, bending to talk into the speaker. "We're having technical difficulties right now…" His gaze flicked up to mine, widening slightly at the voice he recognized on the other line. "You'll have to call back later, byyyeee."

I bit my lip to hold in my laughter at his extended bye. Why was everything he did or said so sexy? He picked up the handset and pressed his finger into the cradle to end the call.

"How did you get trapped?" I opened my mouth, but he held his hand up, shaking his head as he said, "Never mind."

His long fingers grazed over my blouse-covered ribs. I sucked in a breath at the contact, willing the shiver that was rolling down my spine to not be so obvious. Axel halted and inclined his head toward me. His thumb hooked under the last part of cord and brushed against my nipple.

He knew exactly what he was doing. The stupid, sexy, man.

"My hero," I whispered.

He placed the handset back and stood straight. "I'll be the Hulk to your Black Widow any day."

I raised a brow, leaned back in my seat, and crossed my legs. His eyes flared at the movement. *Yeah, two can play that game.* "I much prefer Thor and Jane, but okay." I shrugged.

"Thor?" he asked.

"Mmm-hmm." I skimmed my fingers over my knee, pulling the material of the split closer together. I glanced up, held my hands apart in front of me, and gave him a coy look. "He has a very big...*hammer*."

———

I wrapped the scarf around my neck and pulled on my pink mittens that matched my woolen cat hat. I looked cool as shit if I said so myself. I'd finished my last shift at work yesterday, and I wasn't going to lie, I was going to miss the stupid steel and glass building.

It was cold and dark as I stepped out of the hotel and onto the sidewalk, looking left and then right. I spotted Axel who was wearing a big winter coat and a scarf tucked into it but no cat hat—shame, he could have totally worked a hat with ears.

I walked over to him and stopped a couple of feet away, waiting until he ended the call he was on. A grin spread across his lips.

"Hey."

"Hey yourself," I answered, moving closer to him as the wind whipped around us. "What was the big rush?"

"It's Christmas Eve," he told me, like that would answer my question. "It's tradition to go and see the Rockefeller Christmas Tree."

I gasped, backing away a step. "*Noooo.*"

"*Yesss,*" he mimicked, mocking me.

I glared, but I couldn't keep it for long because I was too freaking excited. I jumped up and down, my right arm flapping beside me. At least I remembered not to do it with both arms, so I didn't look like a dancing chicken. The impact of my sneakers hitting the ground vibrated through me, licking pain into my collarbone. I winced and stopped.

"Are we going now? *Right now*?"

"Uh-huh." He held his hand out to me, and I didn't hesitate to put mine into it as he led me from the front of the hotel and down the street.

We walked for about fifteen minutes, conversation flowing freely. It was so easy to be around Axel. Not once did he comment each time I nearly tripped. He simply reached out, stopped my fall, righted me, and took my hand again. That's what I found most sexy about him. It was an automatic reaction. That and he didn't make fun of me.

We turned the corner and there in all its glory was the tree I'd wanted to see my entire life. It was huge. Bigger than anything I'd ever seen, and when I told Axel this, he raised his brow and pointed down to his junk in question.

"Yep." I nodded, chuckling under my breath as I let his hand go and moved closer to it. "Way bigger than that."

"Hey!" I ignored him as his footsteps came nearer, and when he lunged for me, I squealed loud and ran through the gathered people. "You can't run from me, Vi!"

I turned back to face him, grinning as I shouted, "Like Leonardo said: Catch me if you can!"

He raised a brow, quirked his lips, and dove for me again. I spun around and ran, weaving in and out of people who were staring up at the tree.

I backed myself into a corner, but when the lights on the tree flashed, I halted. I stared at them like a baby who'd just been handed his first piece of candy.

"Wow," I whispered in total awe. The different-colored lights flashed on and off, the decorations in proportion to the gigantic tree. I wanted a tree like this in my apartment.

"Gotcha!"

Arms banded around my waist and I screamed, "Duck!"

He ducked his head, his wide eyes searching everywhere around us. What the hell was he doing? "What, Vi? What is it?"

"What the frack are you doing, Axel?"

"You told me to duck."

"Nu-uh, I said…" I lowered my voice so the kids standing next to us couldn't hear us. "I said fuck."

"No, you said duck."

"Nooo… I said—"

"You said duck," an old lady standing next to us interrupted. "My cell always corrects fuck to duck." She didn't lower her voice, so it gained the attention of all the kids.

"I—"

"Thing drives me crazy! If I want to say fuck, then let me say fuck!" She met my eyes. "Am I right?"

"Erm…sure?"

"Damn straight I'm right." She turned away from us, and I glanced up at Axel. He was pressing his lips together, trying to hold in his laughter.

"And don't get me started on it changing bitch to birch! And what's with kids using an eggplant as a penis? It's a goddamn eggplant!"

Axel shifted closer to me, pressed his front against my back, and positioned his hand on my stomach. His long fingers spanned wide, and I sagged against him. There was nothing like the safety I felt when he held me like this.

"I sent one to my friend when she asked me for a recipe, and she messaged back saying, 'Doris, if you want a dick then head downstairs, I'm sure the ninety-year-old man will give you a good seeing to.'"

Axel lost his battle at the woman's rampage about autocorrect and emojis and hid his face in the crook of my neck.

"Oh my God," I whispered and covered my mouth with my hand.

"That was my reaction, too!" She shook her head, her lips pulling up into a sneer. "I'm seventy-nine for God's sake, I don't want no old fart to be putting his wrinkled balls next to my jewelry box."

"Jewelry box?" I asked, cringing as soon as the words escaped my mouth. I should—

"My vagina, dear." She patted my hand as if I was a pre-teen who didn't know what it was.

"Grandma! There you are!" A surfer-looking guy walked up to her and grasped her arm gently. "Have you been causing trouble?" he asked knowingly.

"Me?" Her voice was all innocent now. "I would never cause trouble. I'm an upstanding member of the community." She winked at me as he pulled her along with him. "You make sure you get some of that eggplant tonight." Her head tilted toward Axel and then she was lost in the crowd, leaving me completely speechless.

"Did she just..."

"You know, I quite fancy moussaka right now."

"You can't be serious." I twirled around in Axel's arms.

He shrugged. "All the talk of food has made me hungry." His gaze flicked around the area. "Let's go grab some food and then we can head to the ice rink."

He placed a gentle kiss on my lips, pulled his arms from around me, and grasped my hand again.

"No way." I shook my head emphatically. "I can barely walk on two feet. Ain't no way you're getting me in a pair of skates."

"Don't be a scaredy cat, Vi." He tugged me through the crowd.

"And I have a broken bone, I don't need another!"

Chapter 10

CONFESSION #70: I TRIPPED ON A SOCK, SMACKED MY HEAD OFF THE KITCHEN DOOR AND FELL INTO THE LAUNDRY BASKET FULL OF DIRTY CLOTHES. THIS IS MY LIFE.

"I'm sore in places I didn't know I could be sore," I groaned when I got out of the car, El following me with Chad and Axel.

"Here she goes again." El rolled her eyes. "I've told you: I don't want to hear about my nearly brother-in-law's penis."

"Hardy-har." I grimaced when I moved a step away from the car Axel drove us in. I didn't know why I had this notion that he couldn't drive, but apparently, he could, and he owned an awesome sports car to boot.

"Was she like Bambi?" El asked Axel, sliding up next to Chad.

"Worse." Even he grimaced. He probably thought I was joking about me and skates, but we weren't on the rink for five minutes and I'd already fallen into him a total of thirteen times. At that number, he promptly got me off the ice, telling me it was a bad omen. At least he didn't let me go and kept his arm around me so I didn't fall.

Thank you, broken collarbone.

I strode toward him, wishing we were still in the warmth of his bed, naked and tangled in the sheets while eating pizza and watching a movie. *A girl can dream*. Instead, I was standing in front of a house in the Hamptons complete with a tree in the front yard that could put the one from last night to shame.

"Wow, so your parents are into Christmas, huh?"

"Big-time," Axel answered, setting his arm around my shoulders and being careful of my left one. "Be prepared to not be able to move after this feast and to have gained five pounds."

"It's all good," I told him as we walked up the staircase on the left—yes, the left—side of the front door. "Does your mom know I'm—"

"Children!" a loud voice rang out as the door was thrown open, revealing a woman shorter than me with big puffy hair and wearing a Christmas apron. "You brought guests!"

"Miriam, I'm shocked." El's hand went to her chest in outrage. "I'm not a guest—"

"Yeah, yeah." She waved her away and headed right for me. "I'm talking about this delicious piece of meat."

"Me?" I asked, pointing at my chest and looking up at Axel who was running his hand down his face.

"Don't, Ma…"

"Don't you 'Ma' me," she reprimanded, stopping a pace in front of me. "Don't just stand there," she goaded and opened her arms wide. "Give me some love."

I hesitated which caused her to grab me around the shoulders and yank me to her. I bit my bottom lip to counteract the pain, but it didn't work, and a groan escaped my lips.

"Ma, she has a broken collarbone, I told you this."

Axel stepped behind me and pulled me from his mom's embrace.

"Oh, shucks, of course you did. I must have…" She paused. "I must've forgotten."

The temperature dropped, and Axel's body became taut. I frowned and searched all of their expressions, noting the pain-filled eyes and straight, grim lips. What was I missing?

"It's okay," I told her. "I'd forget my panties if they weren't—"

"Don't finish that sentence," Axel groaned. He let me go and walked past us and into the house.

"What?" I asked. "Was it something I said?"

Miriam chuckled, slipping her arm through mine as she led me into the house. "I have a feeling I'm going to like you."

"Well, thanks." I paused. "Do you have eggnog?"

She scoffed. "Of course, I do."

"Then I already love you," I said, being deadly serious.

She threw her head back and laughed, pushed open a door, and stepped into the biggest kitchen I'd ever seen in my entire life. There were so many cupboards, and the counters gleamed much like the dark, oak wood floor.

"Wow. Do you cook in here often?"

She let go of my arm, and that was when I realized nobody else had followed us in here. Not that I minded, because I was used to being on my own and meeting new people. It wasn't like Axel was my boyfriend and I needed to impress his mom. I could just be me, Vi, the number one klutz in the States.

"I used to," she said, heading toward the refrigerator. "Oh! I wondered where these got to." She pulled a pair of glasses and a jug of something out. "I've been looking for these all morning." She laughed at herself, but it was a sad kind of laugh, one used to ease tension.

She poured two glasses and handed me one, telling me it was eggnog, and as soon as it hit my tongue, I moaned.

"So, Violet. Axel tells me you're heading back home tomorrow. Are you doing Christmas with your family then?"

I swallowed the gulp and cleared my throat. "Ah, no. My parents like to go on vacation at Christmas." I shrugged. "I don't see them often so…"

"There you are," a man with a deep voice said, and when I turned around, I saw a spitting image of Axel, only older with graying hair.

He headed for Miriam, kissed her cheek, took the glass out of her hand, and had a sip. The smiles on their faces and love shining in their eyes spoke volumes.

"They've always been like that," Axel whispered in my ear, wrapping his arm around my waist from behind.

I closed my eyes as I leaned my head against his chest, relishing in the hard planes of his body. This time tomorrow I'd be on a flight back to LA. I didn't want to admit I was going to miss him, but I would. Stupid feelings.

"You must be Violet," his dad announced, causing my eyes to open. I straightened, but Axel didn't loosen his arm.

"I am," I murmured.

"Don't hug her, Marcus! She has a broken collarbone."

He tilted his face toward Miriam, but I saw the smile he pasted on for her benefit. "Okay, love. Luckily you reminded me because I forgot about that." He focused his attention on me, but the sadness in his dark-blue eyes told me he hadn't forgotten about it at all, and he was simply placating her.

He held his hand out to me. "It's nice to meet you."

"You too," I replied, shaking it.

"When's this turkey gonna be done, Ma? I'm starved!" Chad shouted as he entered the kitchen with El beside him.

"Let me check." Her mouth spread into a wide grin as she murmured, "So nice to have both of my boys back in one place."

I tilted my head back and met Axel's gaze. He shot me a wink and planted a kiss on the end of my nose. "You weirdo," I whispered, wiping the kiss away.

He gasped. "You can't wipe my kiss away."

"I can and I will."

He leaned down and kissed me again, except when I went to wipe it away, he held my arm and kissed me several more times. I giggled like a schoolgirl. Inside I was shaking my head at the sound, but I couldn't help it around Axel.

"Where's the turkey?" We pulled apart and spun around at the sound of Miriam's distressed voice. "I know I put it in the oven." She wiped her hand furiously on her apron as she searched the room. "Where is it?"

Axel removed his arm from my waist and paced toward her, holding his hands out. "It's okay, Ma, don't—"

"I put it in the oven, I know I—" She cut herself off as she stared at the sink and the giant turkey sitting in a roasting pan, waiting to go in the oven. "Oh my gosh, I've forgotten to put it in the oven."

"It's okay," Axel whispered. "We can put it in now."

"No! It won't be cooked for another five hours and—"

"We can stay the night." He turned to face me. "Can't we?"

The pleading look in his sad eyes had me nodding. "Of course. My flight doesn't leave until twelve. And I have a feeling I won't be able to move after this feast, anyway."

"Are you sure?" she asked, her voice sounding like a sad child's.

"Of course." I shucked my jacket off. "What can I do to help?"

———

"Wait, wait, wait… Say that again." The grin on my face was hugantic as Miriam laughed at her story.

"It's true." She nodded emphatically. "He swung to hit the baseball, lost his footing, and hit himself in the face with it."

I snickered, turning my gaze to Axel as I raised my brow. "So, you were a klutz, too?"

He took a final mouthful of mashed potatoes and pushed his plate away. "Yeah." He leaned forward, chewing. "But I grew out of it."

"Touché."

Moaning as I put the last slice of gravy-covered turkey in my mouth, I turned back to Miriam. "What other stories do you have about—"

"Nope." Axel stood and shook his head. "That's enough embarrassing stories." He walked around the table and stopped beside me. "Let's start clearing the table before we do presents."

I tilted my head back, smiling at Axel upside down. He grinned back at me, placed his hand on my shoulder, and moved his fingers up to the side of my neck. We stayed like that for a moment, our eyes telling so many things neither of us was willing to acknowledge. I closed my eyes, shuttering it all off, not willing to expose every part of me when I'd be leaving the state in less than twenty-four hours.

We made quick work of clearing the table, working in relative silence. I didn't know what Axel was thinking about, but I knew I couldn't get the amount of time we had left together out of my head.

We finished and headed into the living room where everyone was waiting next to the giant Christmas tree, the lights flashing and twinkling much like the stars in the darkened sky outside.

Axel sat down on one of the sofas, and they started to hand out presents. I shuffled awkwardly. "I need to get my presents—"

"We've already brought them inside," El interrupted.

"Oh." I ambled forward and paused as Axel held his hand out to me. I placed mine in his, relishing in his soft palm as he pulled me down next to him.

Presents were passed back and forth. El loved the new graphics card I got her, along with a bright-pink hard drive. I didn't know what to get everyone else, so I had El help me. Chad got a new ball cap, Miriam a bottle of perfume, and Marcus a pair of slippers. But I knew exactly what to get Axel.

He raised his brow at me as he ripped the paper and I bit my bottom lip. He chuckled. "Fluffy socks?"

"Yep." I reached over and held them up. "I saw these and thought, 'These would be perfect for Axel.'" I paused, my lips quirking. "I see the way you look at mine in the office."

He cupped the side of my face and stared at me. "I'm gonna miss you when you're gone."

I swallowed down the lump starting to build in my throat and opened my mouth to tell him I'd miss him too, but El commented, "I don't get it."

"As soon as Vi gets to her desk, she leans down, pulls off her torture devices—"

"Torture devices?" Marcus asked.

"Heels," I supplied, not looking away from Axel as his eyes sparkled.

"Then she pulls on the brightest fluffy socks I've ever seen. A different pair each day. Striped, neon yellow, green, pink…you name it, she has them."

"It's cold in your office."

The air crackled as he skimmed his fingertips down my cheek. My eyes fluttered closed and a shiver rolled through me. He grasped my chin. "I know it is." He lowered his voice. "Your nipples are a telltale sign."

I gasped. "My nips have been popping out this whole time?"

"Yep." He chuckled, planted a soft kiss on my lips, pulled back, and grabbed a present down by his feet. "I got you this."

"Ohhh!" I snatched it from him and ripped the paper open like a three-year-old kid. It tore every which way, and a frame was revealed. "You didn't!"

"I did."

I lifted my head, snorted at him, and turned the frame around so everyone could see it.

"I figure you're not going to see my face every day, so you might miss my handsomeness."

"Is that right?" I asked as El came closer.

"Mmm-hmm."

I spun the frame back around, looking at the image of Axel dressed in his suit, staring at the camera with a broody expression on his face.

"I also have this to put in the bottom corner."

He reached into his pocket and pulled out a small picture. He placed it in the corner, and I lifted it closer, smiling wide at the photo of us from last night next to the ice rink, me with my cat-ear hat on and Axel standing behind me, his arm around my waist as we both grinned at the camera.

"I love it," I whispered, trying not to choke on the lump in my throat that wouldn't disappear.

He shuffled closer to me on the sofa. "I have another present for later."

"You do?" I asked, lifting a brow at the grin on his face. His hooded eyes trailed over my chest, and I sputtered a breath at the attention.

"I do."

He leaned toward me again and kissed me, only this time wasn't quick like the first time. He savored it, pressing his soft lips against mine slowly and pulled back the smallest of fractions.

"Merry Christmas," he murmured.

"Merry Christmas, ya filthy animal."

———

I stared out of the window as we made our way to the airport, hating I was going to miss the cold weather.

When I landed here eight weeks ago, I couldn't wait for the fifty-six days to be over, but now I wished I didn't have to go back to the sunny state.

I wanted to keep wearing my new hat and gloves. I wanted my feet to be cold while I was sitting at my desk. But most of all, I wanted to be able to look to my left and have instant man candy.

"You good, Vi?"

"Yeah." I nodded and placed my hand over Axel's as he gripped my thigh.

I couldn't stop thinking about the conversation we had last night. He'd told me that his mom had Alzheimer's, and as soon as he'd said that word, it had all made sense. The pain-filled looks they'd given her, the small smiles when she talked about Axel and Chad as kids. But I'd sensed everyone on edge the entire day, waiting for something to happen.

Axel wasn't the kind of person who opened up to just anyone, and yet he'd told me all of his worries when it came to losing his mom. He was afraid of watching her become a shell of a person, and I understood how scary that must be.

When we woke up this morning, something was different in the way he moved and talked. I sensed that he was opening up to me last night and that maybe we were going to be more than what I thought. I really shouldn't have let my mind run away with me though because he obviously hadn't been thinking the same thing. We had eaten a quick breakfast with barely any words spoken between us before we left to get my stuff from the hotel to head to the airport. As if he hadn't confessed his darkest fear to me last night.

El wouldn't come with us, not that I expected her to

anyway because she hated goodbyes. So there was only me and Axel, the man who had surprised me at every turn, taking all of my weird moments in his stride and not once asking for more from me.

Why was that? Maybe he didn't see me as long-term material?

I shook those thoughts from my head as Axel pulled up in the drop-off section and switched the engine off but didn't make a move to get out of the car. It wouldn't work between us anyway on account of the fact I lived nearly three thousand miles away.

Neither of us said anything for a few minutes until Axel cleared his throat. "You'll miss check-in." His voice was flat, and I wondered what it meant.

Maybe he'd ask me to stay? Would I stay in New York if he asked me to?

"I know," I whispered, reaching for the door handle and pushing my brain to the back of my head. Of course he wouldn't ask me to stay. I was a stop gap, something to pass the time. Not that he wasn't the same for me.

Damn, I could feel tears working their way to the front of my eyeballs. I stepped out of the car and halted, working the dates out in my head. Yep, my time of the month was soon. At least it explained why my emotions were all over the place. Silly me for thinking it was something more.

I straightened my back, walked around to the trunk, and lifted the handle on my case as Axel placed it on the ground.

"So…I guess this is it?"

He closed the trunk. "You may see me in LA now and again."

"Right." I nodded, way too many times to look

normal. *Now and again. He definitely wasn't going to ask me to stay.* "I better…" I hooked my thumb over my shoulder and tilted my head to the main doors of the airport.

"Yeah."

I brought my gaze to his eyes, hating how I couldn't tell what he was thinking. I stepped forward at the same time as he did, both of us going in for a hug—me low and him high.

My hand met his junk, but I styled it out by smirking up at him. "Just saying bye to him, too."

He shook his head, chuckling. "I'll miss your awkw—"

"Awesomeness," I interrupted, pulling back. "I know, I'm just too cool for words. But hey, if you get bored, then you know where I work."

"This is true." He leaned against his trunk, pushing his hands into the front pockets of his dark denim jeans.

I stepped back, gripped my case handle in my hand and held my hand up in the Spock sign. "Live long and prosper."

I twirled around, not wanting to hear his reply, and walked into the airport, feeling like the last few weeks were a dream. A dream full of awkwardness and amazing orgasms.

I guessed the trip wasn't so bad, considering my lady garden got a good watering. I snorted at myself as I came to the main airport doors and turned to take one last look at Axel, but he wasn't there.

Of course he wasn't. Rolling my eyes at myself, I twisted around to head back to where I belonged: LA and my small apartment.

Chapter 11

CONFESSION # 42: I CUT MY EYE WHILE
HAVING A CONCERT... ON MY BED.

"Who the hell put so many stairs in here!" I blew out a big breath, trying to get the hair out of my face. Jeez, I needed to work out more. One case plus two flights of stairs and I felt like I was going to die.

My stomach growled as the smell of Chinese takeout wafted around me. Mmmm, I'd missed Mr. Chung's specials. I reached the top of the stairs, heaving huge breaths as I stared down the hallway. There was nothing like home, and home for me was my plants and a tiny apartment.

I grabbed the handle of my case and walked toward the second door on the right. I stared at the 2B attached to it, the white paint fading and revealing the rusted metal underneath. It wasn't the best apartment in LA, but it was all I could afford on my own. I knew I could have easily lived somewhere better with a larger square foot, but it would have meant going back into my parents' fold—*no, thank you*!

My cell pinged for the tenth time in the last couple of

minutes as I pushed open my apartment door. I knew Ella was making sure I'd made it home okay, and considering I'd literally just walked through the door, she could wait a few minutes for my reply.

I hoped my plants were still alive.

"Home sweet home!" I slammed the door behind me, leaned my case against the wall, and threw my Converse off my feet. Closing my eyes, I inhaled a deep breath. I was ecstatic to be home, but I didn't miss the strange feeling crawling through me—something was missing. I wanted to deny what it was to myself even as my eyes opened and my gaze landed on my case.

His photo was inside.

I looked away, but I didn't take anything in because my attention was being forced back to the case. It wouldn't hurt to take a peek, right?

I was kneeling down and unzipping it before I knew what I was doing. Clothes flew out in all directions—I was the throw-things-in, sit-on-your-case, and hope-for-the-best kind of packer.

"Where is it?" I asked myself out loud.

I caressed the smooth, polished frame with the pads of my fingers and slid out the photograph from the luggage. I soaked in the sight of his handsome, broody face in the main picture, and then I glanced at the small photo of both of us in the corner. But I forced myself to look away. I wanted to be the cringy girl who held it to her chest and sighed, but I managed to stop myself—barely. I may be weird, but that was a new low even I wouldn't sink to.

I stood and walked around the small sofa in the living room and past the window that was open a couple of inches. I may have been gone for eight weeks, but I had to make sure my plants got some fresh air, even if Mr. Chung from downstairs came to water them every couple of days.

"Hey there, plants! Did you miss me?" I stroked one of the leaves on my giant houseplant, my gaze wandering to the twinkling stars flashing in the darkened sky.

Why did I feel like a stranger in my own home right now?

I stared out of the window, hoping the universe could give me some answers as to why I felt so weird. I mean, I knew I was weird anyway, but I'd never felt like this before. Maybe it was the change in weather? Yeah, that had to be it.

I tore my gaze away, moved toward the cabinet in the corner of the room, and positioned the frame next to the TV sitting on top of it. Pride of place, perfect for me to sit and stare at him. Pacing backward, it took three steps before the back of my knees hit the sofa. I flopped down on it, still not moving my gaze from the image.

Was I obsessed? Hell yeah, I was. You would be too if you'd had that Adonis inside you, on top of you. Goddamn, it was all I could think about. Maybe I should grab Lucas and—

"What the feck!"

I threw my arms out beside me as I jumped off the sofa, my eyes wide. I spun around and saw…a cat? *A cat!* What the hell was a cat doing in *my* apartment?

"Who are you?" I planted my hands on my hips, giving—I tilted my head to the side, noting the balls —*him* the sternest expression I could muster. "How did you get in here?" He lifted his paw, licked his gray fur, and completely ignored me. "Hey, dude! You're in my place. What gives?"

I kept my attention on him for several seconds, but when he didn't move, my gaze wandered over to the window I left open. Crapstickles. Had he climbed through the small gap? Looking back at him, I found him settling down, making himself comfortable on my sofa. He closed his eyes as if I wasn't even here.

What the hell was going on?

I was in shock. Who broke into someone's place and made themselves at home? This was a misdemeanor! He had to go, *right now*. I didn't want a cat. I'd *never* wanted a cat. Holy flaming cheese monkeys! What if he was already someone's pet? What if there was a little girl who loved him to pieces, crying herself to sleep at night?

I moved closer, trying to get a better look at him. He might have had a tag or something—I mean, that was what people did with pets, right? His eyes opened, watching me cautiously as I moved around him, taking in his disheveled state. His fur was matted in places, and I could practically see his ribs. Was he a stray? My lips twisted on one side. What the hell was I meant to do with a stray cat?

He needed to go. Cats were not my thang. There was only room for one pussy in this apartment.

Reaching my arms out, I stepped closer to him, preparing to remove him when he leaped up and hissed at me. My hand flew to my chest, my heart beating wildly as I stumbled. What the fracking hell? "Okay, okay! Jeez," I placated, my hands out in front of me to try and calm him down. "You can stay…*for now*."

The pinging of my cell ricocheted from my pocket,

distracting me from the intruder. I pulled it out and clicked on the message app without looking away from the creature who was shooting fire at me out of his tiny little eyes—I didn't trust him one bit.

Snapping my attention to my cell, I didn't read all of the messages El had sent. Instead, I shot off a quick reply telling her I was home and I'd call her tomorrow.

"I'm going to bed," I told my new housemate after locking my cell. I pointed at him in warning. "I want you gone in the morning." He settled down, stretched his body out, and closed his eyes. "Well, night then."

I shook my head at myself and the fact I knew deep down I wouldn't make him leave. I was a pushover, what could I say.

———

Running my hand down my skirt-covered thigh, I shuffled on the spot as I waited for the elevator doors to open. My stomach churned, but I wasn't sure whether it was from nerves or the breakfast burrito I ate this morning on the way here. Goddamn cat stalking me and making me give him my breakfast!

It dipped again when the doors opened, almost like I was on a roller coaster—definitely nerves. Smiling politely at the other people inside, I pushed my way in and slipped between a middle-aged man who sneered as I knocked his briefcase and an older woman who smiled politely.

I thought the feeling I had yesterday was because I'd just landed, but when I left my apartment this morning it was tenfold. LA didn't feel like home at all now. They said it was the people who made a home, not the place. Maybe that was what it was?

I felt at home in New York, but it wasn't because of the place, it was definitely the people. It was Ella—and maaaaybe Axel too. Were those weeks really only a fling? Did they mean something? It wasn't like I was sitting here saying I loved the guy, but maybe I was in *lust* with him?

Shit, I swore to myself I'd never let this happen. I was an independent woman, dammit. I didn't need a man for anything—not even orgasms. I could put up a shelf as well as any dude, and don't get me started on my hammering skills. *No pun intended.*

As soon as the doors swooshed open, I was staring at the big silver letters of "Taylor Industries." Why did seeing his name on the wall make me feel like I was going to turn the corner and see his face? Gosh darn it! Now I was feeling all discombobulated. I blamed Aunt Flow who'd decided to make an appearance this morning. It was all her fault. She was the reason I was a big fat baby right now. Someone give me a giant bar of chocolate, pleeease!

"Are you getting out?" the man with the briefcase grunted.

"Oh, yeah." Stumbling forward, I kept my attention on his name as the doors shut behind me.

I didn't expect Axel to want to marry me, but jeez, he hadn't even messaged to see if I had a safe flight. For all he knew I could be stranded on a mountain in feet of snow like Kate Winslet in her movie with that sexy-ass guy, Idris Elba. A smile worked its way on my lips. I could be with a sexy man right now—great, now Axel's face was in my mind.

"Violet Scott?"

I whipped my head around, frowning at the young woman I'd never seen before.

"That's me," I confirmed with a nod.

"Della wants to see you."

I frowned, completely confused. Why did she want to—ohhhh, the call while I was in New York. "Oh." I took a step toward the part of the floor my station was in, but this whippet of a woman moved in my way. I raised my brows, gawking at her like she was insane. "I'm just going to set my stuff at my station."

Her lips flattened into a thin line, something flashing in her eyes as she tilted her head toward Della's office. "Della's a very busy woman. She asked to see you right away."

I stared at her, trying to decipher anything I could from her expression which wasn't much considering she was stone faced. These last two days had been a constant cause of confusion.

I followed her, taking note of the new desk sitting outside Della's office. The woman took a seat there, picked up the handset on the desk, and talked into it. I stood awkwardly, clutching my purse as I stared at her. She couldn't be more than twenty and seemed to be well out of her element, but the way she sat up straight—I mimicked the action, no slouching here. No, siree!—told me she didn't mess around. That and the desk organization she had going on.

My station outside Axel's office was *never* this tidy. I had little knickknacks on it and Post-it notes stuck everywhere to remind me of things I needed to do. It may not have been like this woman's, but it was my own kind of system.

"You may go in now."

I startled at the sound of her voice, making a little noise in the back of my throat. I pushed my shoulders back, strode toward the door, took a deep breath, and pushed it open. I was blasted by a stone-faced Della, her dark-green eyes flashing as her gaze scanned me from head to toe. The sunbeams shone through the floor-to-ceiling windows and made her bright-red hair look even shinier. One thought came to mind—she didn't look happy at all.

"Hi," I whispered. Where the hell had my voice gone?

"Miss Scott." She waved her hand to the seat opposite her desk. "Take a seat."

I did as she said, crossing my ankles and uncrossing them as she stayed silent and typed away on her keyboard, her perfectly manicured nails clicking on the keys.

She finally glanced up and narrowed her eyes. "How was New York?" She pasted a smile on her gloss-covered lips.

"It was…good?" I bit my bottom lip. *It was more than good. It was fantastic, amazing, orgasmic—literally.*

"Excellent." She nodded and paused as leaned forward and steepled her hands on the desk. "Do you have anything to report?"

"Report?" I asked, confused—*yet again.*

"Yes. I want to know how the New York office is doing…and, of course, Axel." *Axel?* I stared at her, my brows drawing down. She seemed to read my expression because she expanded, "Axel and I met in college." There was something in the depths of her eyes that told me she was trying to say more than she was actually vocalizing. "How is he?"

"She's trying to get her own back for me sleeping with her senior year." Axel's voice sounded in my head and it clicked: *they slept together!* Ewwww. Fucking…ewwww.

"Erm…he's okay?"

She blew out an audible breath and glanced out the window. "I bet he's running around sleeping with anything with a vagina, huh?" She laughed, but it was brash, uncontrolled, so much unlike the boss I knew. Wait a minute…

Was she hung up on Axel?

She fiddled with the sleeve of her blouse, tugged on it, and ran her fingers through her hair. *Holy shit. She was.* My eyes widened at the revelation. This didn't bode well for me at all.

"I erm…ah… I didn't see him with any women." I wasn't lying. I really hadn't because the woman was me! Crapstickles.

Her head whipped around, her eyes flashing with a warning. "I don't care if he *is* with any women." She waved her hand through the air, but I could clearly see she was lying. "I want to know if the New York office is running smoothly. The clients, are they satisfied?"

"I mean… I guess so?" I shrugged. "I was only PA'ing so…"

She rolled her eyes. "Well, you've been of no use. You should always keep your ear to the ground, Miss Scoot—"

"It's Scott," I interrupted.

"Sure, sure." She turned her attention back to her computer. "You can go."

I sat still for a second, wondering what the hell

happened just now. Did she send me there to spy on him and the company? Is that why she really wanted me to go because she thought I'd bring her back all the gossip?

Shit. This woman was bonkers.

———

My pen scratched the surface of the paper, my mind somewhere else completely. I didn't know how long I'd been sitting at my desk, I didn't even know what I was drawing until I leaned back in my chair, put the pen down, and stretched my fingers out.

I glanced up and noticed everyone's attention on something behind me. I frowned and turned, being greeted by a red-faced Della and my grinning supervisor, Elliot, who was following her.

Someone was on their shit list.

I turned back around and closed my notebook and moved my mouse to bring my screen to life. A small hand slapped a pile of papers on my desk, startling me. My gaze tracked the hand on top of them, up an arm, and finally to Della's face. Her eyes stayed fixated on mine, her lips lifting into a sneer.

I glanced at Elliot, trying to gage what was happening but he gave nothing away until Della announced, "The contract you signed when you were employed." I flicked my gaze down to it, wondering why she'd slapped it on my desk. She stood straight, crossing her arms over her chest. "Read section four point eight."

I tentatively reached for it. "Why?" She raised a brow, not answering me, so I blew out a breath and picked the pile of papers up, finding section four, and reading it in my head from start to finish. "I don't understand."

"Of course you don't." She huffed, picked up the papers and read, *"Work relations are not permitted. In any instance this happens, the guilty parties' contracts will be terminated effective immediately. Upon signing this contract, you agree to these terms."*

"Okaaay…"

"You broke the contract."

My cheeks heated as she stared at me knowingly. Fuck. She knew I did the feather bed jig with Axel.

"Obviously we can't fire both of you." She searched the area we were in, making sure everyone's attention was on her. Her lips quirked on one side, and she raised her voice. "On account of the other party being your *boss* and the *CEO* of this company. But you? I *can* fire you."

"What?" I whispered. "I—"

"Don't try and play me, little girl," she practically growled, leaning down and getting in my face. "You think I don't have my spies in New York? I suspected something yesterday when you were cagey about Axel." Her eyes flashed. "But now I know for sure. I know where you were for Christmas. I know what you did with Axel. I know it all."

"No, you—"

"He told me." I reeled back, my eyes widening as she straightened again, her lips now encased in a smug smile. "He told me *everything*. Why do you think that is?"

"He…he wouldn't." *Would he?*

She cackled a laugh, her head thrown back. "Of course he would! It's what he does. He had his fun with you and knows he needs to get rid of you. You're working for his company—he doesn't need it to come back on him."

"Doesn't need what to come back on him?" I asked, almost afraid.

"Listen, Violet." Her tone was placating, but I saw the raging bitch behind her perfect exterior. "You aren't the first person he's done this to, and I'm *positive* you won't be the last." She shook her head. "I should have known he'd do this when I sent you to New York. He hasn't changed one bit since college."

I knew there was more to it, I could feel it deep within my bones, but right now my pride had been wounded. I needed to say or do something, but my mouth wouldn't open.

"You didn't really think he liked you, did you?" She stared at me, her beady, green eyes scanning my face. "Oh, gosh, you did!"

"Cut the fucking act," I growled, reaching my boiling point. Finally, my mouth started working! "You're so full of shit, I don't believe a word that comes out of your mouth." I shoved my pad in my purse, threw the strap over my shoulder, and stood. "This job sucks anyway!"

I stomped over to the elevators and jabbed my finger on the button.

"Try calling him and see what happens! You'll have all the answers you need."

I twisted my body to face her and the floor full of faces with all their attention on the show in front of them. She'd just achieved exactly what she'd set out to do: embarrass the shit out of me.

The elevator doors pinged, and I lifted my lips up into a sneer. There was no way I'd let her know how mortified I was right now. I twirled around, stepped into the elevator and kept my back to them as the doors closed.

What the hell was I going to do now?

My mind was on overdrive, and nothing was computing. She couldn't be right. There was no way Axel would do this to me. He knew how much I needed this job. Not only that, but El would have killed him before I even got the chance to step foot in New York and do it myself.

I staggered out of the elevator and didn't stop—on a mission. I was so angry. I couldn't believe she'd fired me in front of the whole floor!

Pulling my cell out, I then dialed his cell number. When I didn't get an answer, I tried his office number.

"Mr. Taylor's PA—"

"Hi, I'm Violet Scott, please put me through to Axel."

There was a pause, and then the voice replied, "I'm sorry, he's really busy right now—"

"I don't give a flying duck if he's busy, I want to talk to him *right now*."

"Umm…I… Okay."

There was some shuffling over the line, and then it was connected, and his voice gritted out, "What?"

"Axel?"

I heard his low breath and my spidey sense kicked in. Was she right? Did he really do this? Did he really get me fired? "I can't talk right now, Violet."

Violet. He used my full name. Not Vi—Violet.

"I need to—"

"Didn't I tell you I was busy, Amber?" he snapped.

"I know, sir, but she seemed—" the new PA answered him.

"I don't care how she seemed!" *Oh. Wow.* "I have a deadline, and this has—"

Their voices stopped, and I pulled the cell away from my ear, seeing the call had dropped.

He hung up on me!

"Mothertrucker!"

Chapter 12

CONFESSION #13: I FELL INTO A BUSH IN SLOW MOTION... A GREEN BUSH, NOT A DOWNSTAIRS BUSH.

I pushed my way through the main door between the Chinese takeout and small grocery store, stomped up the stairs avoiding the yellowing walls and down the small hall housing three doors for the apartments.

Apartments was a word I used loosely. It was basically one room with partitioned spaces and a door for my bathroom. I didn't live in the land of luxury, but right now I was lucky to even have that.

Fired. Again.

Godfuckingdammit!

This time it wasn't my fault. Oh, no, no, no. It was *hers*. By hers, I meant my vagina, my dick hole, my pussy, my meat flaps, whatever the hell you wanted to call it. I opened my door and sneered at my vagina. If she had just kept herself under control, I wouldn't be in this position right now.

The door vibrated shut behind me as I slammed it closed and I stood still, my gaze roving over the room. Small sofa, coffee table in front of it, windows to the right between the sofa and the "kitchen" which consisted of three cupboards and one counter with a bar stool tucked underneath it. To the left was a curtain partitioning off my bed and a chest of drawers. And that was it. My sorry excuse of a life.

Okay, okay, so I was having a pity party, but I was allowed!

Yanking my hair tie out, I shook my hair and tossed my purse down onto the sofa. Pushing through to my small bathroom, I then took my contacts out with much more force than I should have and threw my glasses on my face—figuratively, not literally. My skirt was next to go, along with the stupid blouse, and then I was left standing in my panties and brace.

I was a sorry excuse for a woman right now, and I couldn't help stepping closer to the mirror that hung on the back of the bathroom door to analyze myself. I looked the complete opposite of how I'd appeared and felt only last week—defeated.

Back then I was lying in Axel's bed, his muscly arms wrapped around me, his boner prodding my ass cheek, and his sexy voice whispering sweet nothings in my ear. But that was exactly what they were: nothings. Now I was more or less naked with no job and rent due in two weeks.

It was official: I sucked at adulting.

"Hey, Soul Sister" started playing from the living room, and I sighed because I knew who it was from the ringtone. I honestly didn't think I could talk to her right now, so I left it as I plopped down on the side of the tub, the cold seeping through me and making goose bumps spread over my skin.

When would I be able to do something I loved? Something I was passionate about and couldn't see myself doing anything else? When would it happen for me? When would it click what I was meant to be?

They said your job didn't define you, but what happened when you had no clue what you were meant to be doing? Yeah, you shouldn't be just what you do, but I needed clarification, dammit!

Violet Scott, tightrope walker—I could barely walk on solid ground.

Violet Scott, teacher—sure, because I couldn't control my own life, never mind a bunch of kids.

Violet Scott, fire thrower—yep, if you wanted me to set fire to everything in my path.

Violet Scott, blogger—and I'd write about…about how *not* to be an adult, because I was doing a shitty job of it right now.

I could go on for days, but not one of them were me.

I saw an article last week advertising for professional mourners. Maybe I could do that? I certainly had the sad expression down pat. Seventy dollars to go to a funeral for two hours and pretend to mourn the deceased. Actually, that was depressing. I'd mark that one off my mental list as a firm no.

The music played again, and I gave up, pushed off the tub and then headed into the living room, not caring that I was walking around nearly naked at 10:00 a.m. Who the hell cared? Not me, that was for sure!

"What?"

"Hello to you, too."

I huffed out a long, tired breath. "Sorry, El. I'm having a bad…*life*."

She chuckled, but when I stayed silent, she cleared her throat. "Vi? What's up?"

I waited, the silence stretching between us and then I

blurted it out. "He got me fired!" I waved my arm about, cringing at the small twinge in my shoulder at the force.

"Wait, what? You got fired?"

"Yep." I flung myself down on the sofa, pulling my trusty blue blanket over me. "Della announced I slept with Axel in front of *everyone*. Said I'd broken the contract I'd signed or some shit."

"Huh?"

"No work relations, you dur dur!"

"Ohhhh…wait, does Axel know about this?"

"Yep." I side eyed the frame sitting next to the TV. His perfect face and stupid eyes watched me as if he was here in the room. I stood, took the three steps to get to the cabinet, and pushed it down so I couldn't see his face. "She told me to call him, so I did, and guess what? He hung up on me! So, yeah, the asshole knew."

"Hot damn, I'm gonna kick his ass!"

"There's no point." I closed my eyes and scrubbed my hand down my face. "I just need to forget these last few weeks happened. Start over like I always do."

We're both silent as I sat back down on the sofa and sunk into the cushions.

"What are you gonna do now, Vi?"

"I have no fucking clue," I groaned.

"What about…what about doing something with your art?"

I scoffed. "My art?" I opened my eyes and zoned in on one of my notebooks sitting on the table in front of me. "We've been through this before. I can't earn a living from my art. They're just silly drawings."

"Silly drawings that are awesome! Of course you could do something with them. I have an author I'm working with right now who's looking for an illustrator. I could—"

"Nope." I sat up. "I'm not doing it, El. I'll figure something out."

"But—"

I needed to shut her down, knowing she wouldn't stop going on about it. Every single time I got fired, I had the same speech from her. "I gotta go."

"Vi—"

"Talk to you later."

I ended the call and switched my cell off. Any other time I would have felt guilty, but right now I wasn't in the mood to listen to her. I wanted to wallow in self-pity. Self-pity and ice cream. Now *that* was a solid life plan.

Who needed a job or a man when you had ice cream? Not this girl.

———

I watched Amanda as she opened her eyes, the music in the background starting to choke me up. She whispered Dawson's name as he appeared, and a noise escaped my throat.

Every damn time I watched this movie I sobbed harder and harder.

The scene changed: Dawson talked on his cell, and then the train went by, and I leaned forward. "No!" I shouted when a bullet hit him in the chest, and my hand extended as if I could stop it, even though I knew it was coming. "They were meant to be forever loves!"

It flashed in and out; Dawson dying, Amanda breaking down, and I sobbed like a big old baby.

I couldn't even cope when she got to his place and

read the letter he'd left for her. I was a ball of emotion, and I seriously shouldn't have watched this movie, feeling the way I did right now. *The Best of Me* always gave me the feels.

As soon as the credits rolled, my attention snapped to the picture of Axel and me. I couldn't look away from his stupid face, zoning in on those broody eyes. They held laughter and gentleness when he was focused on me. At least, they *used* to.

The thought of him glancing at me like any other random person wounded me, so I dug my giant serving spoon—the kind your mom used to dish up everyone's food—into my huge tub of ice cream. Ain't got no time for those "normal" spoons and "normal-sized" tubs. I brought it to my lips and opened my mouth impossibly wide to fit the start of the spoon inside. The cookie dough–infused goodness hit my tongue, and I moaned at the taste.

Ice cream always made me feel better.

This was now day five of not leaving my apartment and staring at Axel's picture—I meant the TV. Dammit! What was wrong with me? I needed to get over this. It was a few weeks of fun. *Fun that cost you your job.*

I rolled my eyes at myself as I switched the TV off and put the lid back on the tub of the last little bit of ice cream. Damn, I'd have to go out to get more soon. How did ten tubs disappear so fast?

My gaze explored the open window, and I sneered at the bright-blue sky. Didn't the universe know my life was falling apart? No job. No hanky panky. No drawing. The last one was the worst of them all. I hadn't been able to draw a single thing since I got off the phone with Ella.

"You won't leave me alone, will you?" I stroked the

cat who still hadn't left. I thought he was a loyal kind of guy, unlike *some* people. "I know I need to pick myself up and dust myself off, but I just can't this time."

For every other job I'd been fired from, I'd done just that, but something was different this time. I'd allowed myself to get too comfortable, allowing the notion everything was going to be okay. How stupid could I be? I vowed to my parents I could make it on my own when I pulled away from their impossible rules and regulations, but right now, Dad was the only person I could think to go to.

"Maybe he'll help me?" I glanced down at the furry bundle beside me as if he'd answer me. "Yeah, you're right, Dad would want my soul as payment." I snorted to myself because my dad was the devil.

"I'm hungry," I told him, staring down at my sweatpants that had several stains on them. *Meh.* I jumped off the sofa. "I'm going to get takeout from Mr. Chung."

He followed me all the way to the door where I caught sight of myself in the mirror. Holy hell, I looked like death warmed over! Bags under my eyes, skin as pale as a vampire's, and hair you could fry an egg on—it was *that* greasy.

The cat pushed himself against my leg, so I crouched down and stroked his head. "I guess it's just me and you, dude." I tilted my head to the side. "I should name you, huh?" I tapped my finger on my chin, thinking about it. "Colonel Fourpaws! That shall be your name!" I announced like it was the best name in the existence of names.

He purred louder as if he was confirming it, and I smiled wide. "At least someone loves me."

Pushing up, I grabbed my wallet, blew Colonel Fourpaws a kiss, and headed down the stairs. I looked like a homeless chick, but I seriously didn't give a fuck right now. Wallowing was my middle name.

The bell rang out as I pushed open the door and Mr. Chung shouted, "Violet! Not see you long time."

"I know," I replied with a fake smile on my face. "I'm back now."

His dark-brown eyes trailed over me, the small white hat on top of his head skewed to one side. "You in binge marathon?"

"Something like that." I tried to laugh, but the sound made me cringe. "Can I have my usual?"

"Sure, sure. Be ten minutes. I bring to you?"

"Okay." I threw a twenty down on the counter and held my stomach as it grumbled at the smell of what I knew was the most delicious food I'd ever tasted.

Food was the answer to everything. It would make me feel better, even if only for a little while.

———

I ignored the hundredth message Ella sent me as it scrolled from the top of my cell. Every message was the same:

Ella: Stop ignoring me.

Ella: Do something with your drawings.

Ella: Stop ignoring me!

I couldn't deal at the moment. I refused to be an adult. Instead, I was going to sit here and play cat videos on my cell and let Colonel Fourpaws bat his paws at them.

We'd become the best of friends. We ate together, he sat on top of the toilet while I was showering—the perv —and we shared my bed. He was the perfect guy. Didn't answer me back, kept me company, and kept my feet warm at night.

Match made in heaven. Kinda.

The problem? He was a cat, not a man. Ugh. Man equals muscles and penises, which led me on to Axel. And as if he knew where my thoughts were, my cell vibrated in my hand, and Axel's name flashed. Had he known my brain was thinking about him? My eyes widened to epic proportions, my eyeballs sure to pop out of their sockets.

Colonel Fourpaws glanced at me, his head tilted as if he was asking, "Are you going to answer that?"

"No," I answered him, staring at my cell as it continued to ring.

Why was he calling me? It had been a week since I was fired, and *now* he decided to contact me after hanging up on me? Well, he could go suck it. I was an independent woman. I didn't need to talk to him. He was in my past, a past I was never going to think of again.

Yeah, right. That's why his picture was still on my TV cabinet.

The call ended, and as soon as a message displayed with a voicemail, I deleted it. I didn't want to hear what he had to say. Fuck him, fuck Della, and fuck my stupid heart that begged to hear his voice.

My life was a goddamn mess.

Chapter 13

CONFESSION #92: I KNOCKED MYSELF OUT GETTING INTO BED.

"Your X-ray looks good." Doctor Nick showed me the image on his computer screen. "How is your pain?"

"Not too bad, to be honest," I replied, leaning back in the seat and hoping like hell I could finally get this brace off.

"Good." He clicked on his keyboard, twirled around in his chair, and pushed closer to me. "Let's get this brace off you."

I could already hear my boobage screaming, "No!" at the thought that they had to be put back into a bra, but I outwardly grinned and shouted, "Awesome!"

He smiled gently, his dark-brown hair flopping over his forehead as he nodded. "Do you think this year could be a better year? Maybe only one or two trips to the ER?"

I chuckled. "I'll try." Shrugging—thank the good Lord it didn't hurt now—I stood. "I can't promise anything, though. We all know what a nightmare I am."

He stood with me, and we both moved behind the curtained-off area in his office. "All you can do is try." I heard the laughter in his voice, but I knew there was concern behind it. "At least you went to a different hospital for this one."

"True...although they still mentioned the number of times I've been to the ER."

He washed his hands in a small sink and stepped toward me. "They have to cover their bases."

"I know," I replied, cringing at the thought of taking my top off. I didn't exactly look the best, but that was what ten days of vegging out and minimal showers did to you.

I was coming out the other end now though, I even did some drawing last night. It may have been an ax in Axel's head with blood spurting everywhere, but I was drawing again so who cared what it was of?

I lifted up my T-shirt and spun around so he could get to the buckle. He undid it, and I let it drop off my arms. I rolled my shoulder back and heaved a sigh. The freedom was unreal. I wanted to jump up and down, but I knew it wouldn't be a good idea. The chances of falling over were high, so I kept my feet firmly planted on the floor.

"God, that feels so good."

"I imagine it does."

I put my T-shirt back on, turned, and grinned at him. "Thanks, Dr. Nick."

He pushed the curtain back and shook his head. "I still don't know why you call me that."

I huffed out a breath. "I tell you every time." I planted my hands on my hips. "It's from *The Simpsons*!"

He chuckled lightly as he made his way back to his desk and I collected my purse. "Never watched it."

My eyes widened, my mouth opening and closing like a fish. "You…what?"

He grinned. "I'm not into cartoons."

"Oh, man, you're seriously missing out. Watch an episode, and when I have my next disaster, you can tell me what you think."

He chuckled. "Deal…as long as you try and leave at least three months before the next *disaster*."

"Deal!" I shook his hand, but I knew for a fact that I'd be back before that. It was inevitable, really.

"You're a one-of-a-kind patient."

"I'm a one-of-a-kind person, Doc." I grinned wider, twirled on my heels, and headed to the door, throwing, "See you soon," over my shoulder.

I said my goodbyes to the receptionists and passed through the doors and into the LA heat. I had a love-hate relationship with the sun here. Some days I wanted it to seep into my skin, while other days I wished it was cold and raining so I could curl up on my sofa. Not that I didn't do that anyway, but you got the idea.

I started walking back toward my apartment. Today was a good day. I had my veg fest, but it was time to get back to my life. And the first thing on my list was to get some proper cat food. I couldn't keep feeding Colonel Fourpaws tins of tuna. It was costing a bomb.

I searched on my cell for the nearest pet store and found one a couple of blocks from my apartment. Throwing on my sunglasses, I then pushed my cell into my purse and headed toward the store, surprised when I was greeted with the small front. I'd always imagined pet stores to be these giant places, but from the outside, it looked like it was tiny.

A bell rang as I pushed the door open, signaling a

customer. My nose wrinkled up as soon as I stepped inside, the smell of pet food and hay hitting me full force. I glanced left and right, not seeing anyone, so I decided to go exploring.

The cages toward the back gained my attention and, before I knew it, I had several puppies whining in unison. "Awwww!" I scurried toward them, my hands making grabby motions. I wanted to pick them all up and bury my head in their silky, soft fur. Could a girl get inside one of these cages with them and hang out?

"This breed is perfect for single humans."

My head whipped around at the deep voice, and came face to face with a guy a foot taller than me wearing a polo shirt with a badge pinned to his shirt that read, "I'm Jeffery Junior, how can I help you today?"

"Single humans? As opposed to single…aliens?"

He shuffled on the spot, his green eyes focused on me. "Aliens wouldn't have pet dogs. They'd have—"

I chuckled, cutting him off. "I'm just messing with you, JJ."

His eyes narrowed as he scanned my face. "You have pretty eyes."

"I…thanks?"

"You're welcome." He nodded to himself and moved closer, patting one of the puppies on the head. "What do you want today?"

"Erm…" *What did I come in here for?* "Cat food."

"Do you own a cat?" he asked as he walked away.

I followed him. "No, I wanted to try it and see what it tastes like."

"You won't like it." He came to a stop at the end of the second aisle. "Cat food is there."

"Okay, thanks." I stepped past him, frowned, and turned back to face him. "I didn't really mean I'd eat it."

He shrugged. "Some people like it. I don't."

"Right." I tilted my head, staring at him and seeing the completely serious look in his eyes. "Well, I own a cat. His name is Colonel Fourpaws."

He nodded in reply, but he didn't say anything, so I twirled around. I crashed into the end display and tried to catch it, but all the cat treats scattered along the floor. I stared in horror as the cardboard unit wobbled precariously and promptly crashed to the left.

"Oh, shit!" I scrambled to the floor, trying to pick them all up. "I didn't see it."

"Because you weren't looking," Jeffery Junior scolded. "You should look where you're going, or you could get hurt."

"Son?" a deep voice called. "You okay?"

Footsteps neared as we picked up the treats. Jeffery made a neat pile while I leaned forward and scooped as many as I could toward me in one big swipe. A shadow fell over us, and when I peered up, I was greeted with an older version of Jeffery Junior.

"Yes, Dad. She wasn't looking where she was going and destroyed my display."

My brows raised and I was about to open my mouth to reply when his dad said, "I'm sure she didn't do it on purpose. Remember what I said about accidents?"

His dad smiled kindly at him, then me, and ran his hand through his sandy-blond hair.

"But—"

"Why don't you organize your display again and I'll help this lady find what she wants?"

Jeffery Junior side eyed me, his arms full of cat treats. "Fine. She wants cat food."

"Okay then." His dad walked past us. "I'll show you what we have."

"I…" I handed the treats to JJ and stood. "I'm sorry."

"You should be. It's not kind to destroy people's hard work."

My face heated at his honesty and I backed away slowly, turning around and looking *where I was going*. "I really didn't mean to," I told his dad when I came to a stop next to him.

"It's okay, Jeffery doesn't understand social situations. You're fine."

"Oh… I…"

"So, cat food?" His kind green eyes met mine.

"Right, yeah. So this cat kind of turned up and won't leave. I think he was a stray, and I don't know what to feed him."

He started to explain all the different kinds of cat food, and I decided to go with pouches. "You're better off buying a big box of them. More for your money."

"I'll do that then," I replied as he plucked one up off the shelf and started striding out of the aisle. I stood awkwardly at the counter, pulling my cell out as I waited for him to ring me up. Swiping off yet another message from Axel—the third one today—I let out a long breath. I didn't give a rat's ass what he had to say. He betrayed me. Had this been in the days of Vikings, he'd have his head chopped off.

Mmmm, Vikings…

Shaking the sexy Viking images from my head, I clicked out of the message app, heading into my settings and blocking his number. There! That'd teach the poobrain.

Grinning wide, I clicked on an email from an address I didn't recognize, frowning as I read it. *She didn't. She wouldn't have.*

We would love to see more of your designs. Please email with examples so we can review them and discuss if you would be a good fit at FGT Publishing.

She totally did!

I was going to kill her—slowly—and watch with a grin on my face. Why the hell would she do this to me?

"That's fifteen dollars."

I startled at the voice causing my cell to slip out of my hand and crash to the floor.

"You really need to be more careful," JJ said from behind me.

I bent down and picked it up, and caught sight of the sign attached to the front of the counter. "You need help?" I asked, shooting back up into a standing position. "I mean…you're looking for help?"

"We are," his dad said, leaning his hands on the counter. "I'm Jeffery Senior, and this is my store."

"Can I get an application form?"

His brows lowered. "Can you work a till?"

"I can."

"Can you clean?" I nodded. "Jeffery? What do you think?" I swung my gaze his way.

"She seems nice." He shrugged. "She has pretty eyes."

"You're hired!"

"I am?" My eyes widened as I faced Jeffery Senior.

"You are." He smiled wide. "Jeffery, can you open the delivery that just arrived?"

"Okay." Jeffery wandered off, leaving me and…*Jeffery*.

"My son works here a couple of days a week. As long as you don't get offended by his brutal honesty and can learn to communicate with him on his level, then we can get you started as soon as possible."

"Is he…" I bit my bottom lip, stopping myself from asking something I probably shouldn't as I waved my hand in the air. "Never mind. I can start tomorrow?" My stomach fluttered at the possibility of having a new job. It may only be a pet store, but it was more than I'd had this morning.

"We'll see you tomorrow." He pushed the cat food forward, and I handed him a twenty. "Ten sound good?"

"Ten sounds awesome!" I yanked the box off the side, heaving at the weight. "Keep the change, and thank you so much, Jeffery!"

The grin on my face couldn't be wiped off, not even when I knocked another display over on my way out of the shop.

I hoped they were ready for the disaster that followed me.

———

"Finally!"

"Finally?" Ella sneered down the line. "You turn your cell off and don't answer my calls or texts for *two* weeks, and then send me a message in the *middle of the night* telling me you're going to kill me and expect me to answer right away?"

I threw my arm out beside me, startling Colonel Fourpaws. "Well, what do you expect when you send my drawings to a publishing company!"

"First off, I didn't send them."

I raised off the bar stool. "Then who the hell did?" I started pacing across the small space between the living room and kitchen, Colonel Fourpaws' head followed my every movement like I was his favorite TV show.

"My client."

"What?"

"You need to chill out, Vi. You'll give yourself a heart attack."

"No...*no*, I don't need to chill out. You have no right sending my drawings to your client! How the hell did you get ahold of them?"

There was a pause, and then, "I took pictures of them."

"Fuck me sideways." I let my head drop. "I can't believe you're doing this to me!"

"Wait! If you're pissed, then it means they want to see more." I stayed silent, rolling my lips between my teeth. "They do, don't they? They want to see more of your drawings! This is fantastic, Vi!"

I halted and whined, "No, it's not."

"Hell, yeah, it is!" El shouted. "I knew you'd be a hit! Have you sent more?"

I groaned, flopping down onto the sofa. "No."

"Do itttt!"

I grimaced. "No."

"Stop being a baby, Vi! Pull up those big-girl panties and send them."

"I don't want to."

I stared at the wall, my eyes narrowed. It may have been my dream to draw when I was a kid, but that notion wasn't feasible. People didn't earn a living from drawing unless they were amazeballs.

"You have nothing to lose," El said in a softer voice. "You send them, and if they say you're not for them, then you haven't lost anything, but what if they want you? Look at what you'd gain."

I closed my eyes. "They're in New York," I whispered.

"So?"

I blew out a breath. "I don't want to run into him, El."

"New York's a pretty big place, Vi. Besides, Axel said—"

"Nope, not going there with you." I sat up. "I've gotta go, I got a new job."

"You did?"

"Yep, at a pet store. I went in for cat food, and they offered me a job."

"Cat food? Why the hell were you buying cat food?"

I glanced over at Colonel Fourpaws and rolled my eyes. "Because I have a cat, duh." I stood. "Chat later."

I pressed the end call button and ran my palm over Colonel Fourpaws' back. "I'll see you later, dude. Wish me luck on my first day."

Chapter 14

CONFESSION #30: I TRIED TO DO A "MARY POPPINS" JUMP... WHILE DRUNK. I BROKE MY FOOT BUT CONTINUED PARTYING INTO THE NIGHT BECAUSE... ALCOHOL.

"Puppies need to walk five minutes for every month they've been alive."

"Really?" I turned my head to face JJ—Jeffery Junior. These daily puppy walks were by far my favorite part of the day. What person didn't love playing with puppies and getting paid for it?

"Yep." He nodded emphatically. "These puppies are three months old, so they need to exercise for fifteen minutes."

"Wow, I never knew that." The more I got to know JJ, the more I understood how he thought. He was linear, no gray, only black and white. His honesty was refreshing, and I'd found myself looking forward to his assessments.

We both became silent as we strode behind the six puppies, them sniffing everything in sight and trying to eat leaves. It had been three days since I started working in the pet store, and it was a nice change of pace. No death traps for heels allowed here, thank the good Lord!

"You're thinking."

"I am." I chuckled.

"No, you've been thinking for days. Dad always asks if I want to talk about it…" JJ glanced at me out of the corner of his eye. "Do you?"

"I…" I worried my bottom lip. Right now JJ was one of my only friends. How sad was I to only have one friend here in LA? "I draw—"

"I know. I saw your notebook." He turned to face me. "My favorite is the man with an ax in his head."

"JJ! That's private!"

"If it's private, you shouldn't leave it where anyone can see it."

I rolled my eyes, partly at him, but partly at myself. "Yeah, okay." I scrubbed my hand down my face. "Anyway. My cousin—well, her client—sent my drawings to a publishing company and they've asked to see more, but I'm…" *What the hell was I?*

"Scared?" JJ supplied.

I shrugged. "I guess."

"You should send them. They're good." He said it so simply as if it was as easy as washing your hands.

"I dunno."

"Then don't send them," he replied, his voice level and his focus on the path between the two grassed areas.

"But if I don't send them, I'll never know what could've happened." I looked down at the puppy on the leash in my right hand. "I just don't want to go back to New York."

JJ was silent as we strode a few more steps to the bench he always stopped at for a five-minute rest. He started the timer on his sports watch as I sat beside him. "New York is noisy," he stated.

"It is…it's also home to doucheturd."

"Doucheturd?"

"Yep." I nodded. "But then I shouldn't let him dictate what I want to do. If I want to be an artist, then I have to do it...but...ugh." I dropped my head into my hands. "I'm driving myself insane."

"You're at an impasse."

I lifted my head and leaned back on the bench, the coolness seeping through my thin T-shirt as I stared up at the bright-blue sky.

"I am." I moved my neck so I was facing JJ. "What would you do?"

"I can't draw."

"But if you could?"

"I can't, though."

I chuckled under my breath. "Okay, let's say... someone wants you to help them collect Star Wars figurines—you're good at finding them, right?"

"Yes."

"Okay, so would you? If they paid you, would you do it?"

"Yes."

"Okay..." I rolled my lips between my teeth. "So, you think I should send the pictures?"

"Time's up." JJ stood, skirting his gaze to mine as if silently telling me to get up.

"I think I should send them. Fuck doucheturd, he can go lick a dirty floor."

"Why would someone lick a dirty floor? That's disgusting."

I threw my head back, brash laughter escaping my throat. "It's an expression, JJ."

"It doesn't make sense, though."

Grinning, I tilted my head toward the end of the

park. "Come on, let's get back and I'll send an email before I change my mind."

———

Press send. *Press send.*

Dammit. I couldn't press it! Why the hell was I so nervous? They'd already seen some of my drawings. My skin heated to epic proportions and my hands started shaking as my breath sawed in and out of my chest. I was such a freak! It was an email, and I was about to have a panic attack.

I leaned forward and banged my head over and over again on the small table in the break room. I'd been back from the walk for five hours, and I'd just cleaned the puppies' kennels and closed the shop, and yet I was still sitting here being an absolute pussy and not able to press send.

Why couldn't I do it? Why couldn't I take the next step and try to better myself? "You can do it, Vi. You. Can. Do. It."

I lifted my head, took a deep breath, and stared at the screen of my cell with wary eyes. Bringing my hand closer, I stretched my finger while tilting my head away in slow motion and pressed send.

I did it!

I jumped off the chair and started to dance. My hips moved to an erratic beat of their own, my feet turning to do the running man. "I'm the best! I did it! Helllllllls to the yeah!" I fist-bumped the air, squealing like a little girl.

It was such a small thing but, since I was sixteen, El had been nagging me to send the drawings, and I never had. Planting my hands on my hips, I thrust the air until my cell pinged and I became as still as a statue.

Is that them already? It can't be...can it?

I tiptoed toward the table, gingerly picked up my cell, and let my body deflate when I saw El's name pop up.

Ella: Chad is annoying me... I wanna throat punch him.

Me: Uh-oh, what's he done this time?

I grabbed my purse while I waited for her to reply, switched the lights off, and headed toward the front door.

Ella: He won't let me watch Outlander while I work. Doesn't he know I need to see me some Scottish hottie? Ugh!

A chuckle escaped my lips as I locked the door behind me. I breathed deep, sighed as the evening warmth soaked into my skin, and strolled toward my apartment a couple of blocks away.

Me: Can't you play it on your iPad and let him have the TV?

Ella: And let him win? HELL TO THE NO!

Ella: What you doing? Distract me from being violent.

Me: Just walking home. Guess what?

I grinned, knowing her reaction would be much the same as mine was when I'd finally pressed send.

Ella: What? Tell meeeee.

Me: I sent them…the drawings.

Not five seconds later my cell was ringing with Face-Time, and I clicked accept, a wide smile on my face as soon as it connected.

"You did? You sent them?"

"I did." I nodded, my grin widening. Her face was comical—her eyes wide, her mouth opening and closing like a fish. She seemed to pull herself out of whatever trance she had been in with a shake of her head and jumped up on her sofa. "This is unreal! You're gonna get the job for sure, and then we'll be living in the same city! Ahhhh!"

I chuckled nervously. "Don't get ahead of—"

"Who's moving to the same city?"

El rolled her eyes and glanced to the side. "Mind your own business, *Chad*."

There was a knock in the background, some shuffling, and then the screen filled with darkness.

El growled, "You didn't tell me he was coming over."

"I didn't know you were going to FaceTi—"

"It doesn't matter, I'll go in the bedroom."

I arrived at the corner of my street when she lifted the cell back up. "Everything okay?"

"Yeah, yeah." Her gaze darted to the left as she stood. "We have a visitor and—"

"Is that Violet?" *Shit. Axel.*

My heart beat harder in my chest, and goose bumps spread over my skin like wildfire.

God, how could his voice affect me the way it did? It seriously should be illegal.

"No! It's—"

The cell was plucked out of her hand and then his face came into view, and I didn't know what to do. Did I talk to him? Ask him why he hung up on me after getting me fired? Or did I—

"Vi—"

I squeaked and ended the video call.

I was such a pussy.

"So, you like new job, yes?" Mr. Chung sat behind the counter while on his break, me next to him with Colonel Fourpaws on my lap. One of the downsides to working in a pet store and having a pet meant you spent all your money on stupid things said pet hated.

Every day I came home with something new, but this creation I had on Colonel Fourpaws' body—a small body harness attached to a leash—meant I could take him out with me to visit people.

Coming downstairs when Mr. Chung was on his break and having a chat had become one of our new regular routines. Not that I hadn't use to do this, just not with a cat on my lap.

"Yeah, I love it. Been there for nearly a month now." Colonel Fourpaws' velvety fur grazed my fingers as I stroked his head. "Obviously, I don't want to do it for the rest of my life, but yeah."

"You heard back about pictures?" he asked in his stilted English.

I looked away sheepishly. "Yeah, but... I haven't opened the email."

"Open now."

"I'm—"

"Open now," he repeated.

I lifted my ass off the stool, pulled my cell out, and clicked on the email app. "I'm sure it's a rejection email, anyway. I mean—oh, holy shit!"

"What? What they say?"

My hands started to shake, my stomach dipping with nerves. "They want me to come to New York for a meeting! They love my drawings." I scrolled through the email. "They've sent me tickets to fly first class."

"This good! When you go?"

"Erm... February twentieth...next week." I chewed my bottom lip. "I hope Jeffery will give me the time off."

"He will, he will." Mr. Chung waved his arm in the air. "No worry about that. You worry about finding home for cat while you away."

I blinked. "Oh my God, I forgot about that."

"I have him, but I busy-busy with work."

I smiled gently. "I know, Mr. Chung." I glanced away, staring at the wall. "I'll come up with something."

He patted my arm twice and stood. "I go back work. You want usual?"

"Yes, please."

"You wait. I put chicken in box for cat."

As if he knew we were talking about him, Colonel Fourpaws lifted his head. "Awww, you don't have to."

He waved me away and pushed through to the kitchen in the back.

I started to lift off the stool, except my foot got stuck on the bottom rung as I tried to stand. My arms opened wide, and Colonel Fourpaws flew out of them as I fell facefirst onto the counter.

Why did this feel so familiar?

———

I picked Colonel Fourpaws up off the ground, the leash tangling in his legs. He meowed and wiggled to free himself from the jumble of knots.

"All right, all right! Keep your fur on."

I managed to finally untangle him as I got to the bottom step.

"You're three minutes late."

I startled at the voice and whipped my head up, spotting JJ standing in the doorway to his house. "I know." I ran my hand through my hair. "Colonel Four-paws got distracted."

JJ didn't make a move. He kept his eyes on mine and stated, "You won't be able to leave until three minutes after eight."

"That's fine."

I paced up the steps and onto the wraparound porch. JJ stood watching us, and when he didn't move, I slipped past him and placed Colonel Fourpaws on the floor. JJ closed the door, crouched down, and patted Colonel Fourpaws on the head. He pushed closer to JJ, loving the recognition he was getting.

Colonel Fourpaws was such an attention whore.

I slipped my Converse off, moved closer to them, and undid the leash and collar completely.

"We're having meatloaf."

"Ohhh yum!" I shucked off my jacket and hung it on the small rack next to the door filled with other coats and bags. I placed the leash over the same hook and spun to face JJ. "Do you need help?"

He shook his head as Colonel Fourpaws wandered off. "The table is set, and Dad said it'll be ready in…" He glanced down at his watch. "Seven minutes." He peeked back up at me, and did a double take, his eyes widening. "What happened to your face?"

I skimmed my fingers over the bruise under my eye. "I erm… I fell." I shrugged it off, aware that JJ knew what I was like. I couldn't count the number of times in the past that I'd knocked his displays over.

"Did you seek medical attention?" he asked, his eyes flashing with concern as he lifted his arms and twisted his fingers around one another. "You could have a lesion on your eye, it could make you lose your sight. You have to—"

"JJ." I placed my palm over his large, warm hands, stopping him. "It's okay, honestly. I got checked out."

He let out a deep breath, his gaze not shifting from my eyes as his mouth moved silently. *He's counting, calming himself down.* He twirled around and strode toward the living room, all thoughts of the bruise on my eye forgotten. "I also set a game out. We'll have one hour to play after dinner, and then you have to go."

To anyone else what he was saying would have been abrupt, but to me, it was just JJ. He couldn't understand all social situations and things had to be the right way for him to feel comfortable, but who the hell cared? We'd had customers who looked at him like he was weird. And not the good kind of weird, the *weird* weird kind of weird. He didn't notice the expressions or the snarky comments, but I did, and I wanted to smash each and every one of their faces in. I became She-Hulk when it came to the people I cared about—minus the ripping of clothes and green skin thing.

I shook those thoughts off, followed him into the living room, and sat on the sofa. I'd only just got my ass in the seat when Jeffery shouted dinner was ready. We both made our way to the table, Jeffery at the head with me next to him, and JJ next to me.

This new "Wednesday night dinners," had become a tradition after two weeks of working at the store. JJ adjusted his routine to include me in it, and I couldn't be more grateful. With El in New York, I didn't really have anyone here, so JJ and Jeffery had become like family.

"I've finished," JJ announced, placing his knife and fork on his plate at just the right angle while he waited for us to finish.

"Have you heard back about your drawings yet, Vi?" Jeffery asked, taking a sip of his drink as he glanced at me.

Clearing my throat, I placed my own knife and fork down and straightened in my seat, preparing to ask for time off. "I have." I nodded. "They want me to fly out in just over a week."

"Really? That's great!"

"It is." I winced. "But I need to take some time off to go and... I was wondering if you could look after Colonel Fourpaws, too?"

"Time off is no problem," Jeffery said, finishing up his meatloaf and leaning back in his seat. "JJ, how would you feel about watching Colonel Fourpaws?"

I waited while JJ mulled it over, his gaze batting back and forth between the wall opposite us and the chair in front of it. "How many days?"

I double-checked the email they sent with all the

travel details. "I leave on the twentieth and come back on the twenty-second. So, I could drop him off with you the day before, and pick him up the day after?"

"Five days?" He paused. "I can do that."

"Really?" I smiled wide, stood, and wrapped my arms around JJ's neck. "Thank you, thank you!" His body was as stiff as a board, but I didn't let go. He'd just have to deal with my gratitude.

"It's six forty-five. Time to clean up." JJ pushed his chair back, stood, and stalked from the room. I wondered if maybe I went too far, but when Jeffery smiled at me, I knew I hadn't.

We both headed into the kitchen, and I grabbed a towel, helping dry the plates and pans. We all worked in rhythm, cleaning the place up and keeping an eye on the time. As soon as the hand reached the twelve, signaling 7:00 p.m., we all made our way into the living room to play the game JJ had chosen.

"Awww, man! I love Mouse Trap!"

"Me too," JJ said as he sat on the floor. "Better keep Colonel Fourpaws away." He threw his head back at his own joke, loud, brash laughter pouring out of him uncontrollably. Even though it wasn't your normal kind of joke, I found myself chuckling along with him.

And just as his laughter died off, Colonel Fourpaws strolled in. He stared at each of us in turn and jumped up onto the coffee table, knocking several of the pieces of the game over.

———

When I was certain I had the volume on my playlist turned up to a mind-blowing level, I grabbed the box of supplies and headed toward the back of the store for the night to clean the puppy cages.

I let all the puppies out into the main pen, got down onto my knees—*insert euphemism here*—and sprayed the entire inside of the cages. I was on the third cage across on the bottom row when the bell rang above the door.

"One minute!" I shouted, giving the cage a final wipe and standing up. Swiping the hair out of my face, I walked toward the front of the store, turned the music off, and came to a standstill as the back of a suit jacket came into view. A musky cologne wrapped around me, taking me back to the first time I met him.

I'd recognize that back and cologne anywhere.

What the frack was he doing here?

"Axel?" I whispered, not believing he was standing here—*in* the pet store, *in* LA.

He spun at the sound of my voice, a grin on his face that started to wane when he looked directly at my eye where the bruise had formed. "What happened?" His voice was deep, concern etching its way onto his features.

I lifted my hand to my brow and winced as it throbbed. I let my hand drop as he stepped forward. I was speechless, not able to get a single noise out of my mouth as he raised his hand and cupped my cheek. He grazed the pad of his thumb under the soft skin above my eye where the purple bruise was the worst.

I'd missed his touch and couldn't stop my eyes from closing. A shiver rolled through me, and a sigh slipped from between my parted lips.

"I'm guessing you fell over."

His voice jolted me out of the bubble he'd created,

and my eyes whipped open. What was I thinking? He was the reason I had to work here.

"What are you doing here?"

"What do you think I'm doing here?" he asked as I stepped away from him and wrapped my arms around my waist.

"I don't freaking know, Axel! That's why I'm asking."

He frowned. "You're not answering my calls, and when I turned up at the LA office today, imagine my surprise when Della said you quit."

"What—"

"You didn't have to quit, Vi. If you wanted to put a stop to all this, all you had to do is—"

"Unbelievable!" I threw my arms out wide. "I called you. I goddamn called you to see why you got me fired and you hung up on me!"

His head reeled back. "Wait... What?"

"Don't even act like you didn't. Your new PA put me through, and you called me *Violet*." I sneered my name, staring at him like I wanted to kill him. *Which I kind of did by the way.* "You full-named me!"

"I..." His brow furrowed and he swiped his palm over his jaw. "I did?"

"You did," I confirmed, gritting my teeth.

"I didn't mean to." He let out a long breath, his blue eyes flashing as he looked me dead in the eyes. "I've been busy. Majorly busy. The new contract we worked on came in, and it's—"

"Excuses," I murmured, rolling my eyes.

He jerked forward but stopped himself at the last second. "It's not... I didn't realize—"

"That Della fired me the second day I got back?" I

started pacing along the end of the aisles. "She did it in front of the whole floor. She said I broke the contract by sleeping with a co-worker…" I twirled around, pointing at him. "You. I got fired from *your* company for sleeping with *you*."

"Vi—"

"Then she tells me *you* told her we'd slept together." I stared at him, laser beams shooting out of my eyes. "So, *imagine my surprise*," I mocked. "When you hang up on me and confirm it all!" He opened his mouth, but I cut him off before he had a chance to say anything. "So fuck you, fuck your company, and…*fuck you*!"

"Vi, I swear I didn't know—"

"Of course you didn't," I scoffed.

"Looks like someone forgot the no interrupting rule."

"Yeah, well, I don't work for you anymore so like I said, fuck you."

I crossed my arms over my chest, my eyes narrowed at him, waiting to see what he'd do or say. When he stepped toward me, I mimicked his move backward, causing my back to collide with the counter of the register. His arms came down on either side of me as he dipped his head, his face centimeters from mine.

"Are you done?"

"No—"

His finger pressed against my lips, a ghost of a smile displayed on his face. "I didn't tell her. I didn't know she'd fired you, and most importantly, I can't stop thinking about you."

I wanted to throw my hands up in the air and shout that he was lying, but the honesty in his eyes was all the evidence I needed to see that he was telling the truth. Shit. Did he really not know what was going on?

Ugh. Della was a conniving birch.

"You should seek help, then," I mumbled, still trying to save face.

He raised a brow. "You're on my mind all the time. I look out my office and want to see your face. I get into bed at night and wish your body was against mine." He let his finger drop from my lips. He gripped my hip and moved even closer to me. "You're driving me insane from thousands of miles away."

"Well…" I cleared my throat. "I haven't thought about you at all," I announced, the bitchy tone in my voice evident.

"Liar." He nuzzled my neck, bringing his lips to my ear. "I can't stop, even if I wanted to. I need you, Vi. I need you in my life because without you in it, it's all darkness. You're my light, and I need you to shine bright."

I snorted at his corny little speech. "Where did you get that from? A Hallmark card?"

He leaned back, his lips spreading into a grin. "Maybe."

I shook my head, not able to stop my responding smile. "Okay, I may have missed you, too. But I'm mad at you. Madder than the Mad Hatter."

He stepped away, leaving some space between us. "I swear, I didn't know she was going to fire you, Vi. I wouldn't have let her if—"

"It doesn't matter now," I told him, knowing I was much happier working here than chained to a desk all day.

The silence wrapped around us, becoming thick with tension as he took another step back and pulled on the cuffs of his suit jacket. Was the great, almighty Axel Taylor nervous?

I shuffled on the spot, my hands clutching the counter. "So…"

"So."

I rolled my eyes. "You came here to see me, you saw me, so…you can go now."

"No, I can't." He ran his hand through his hair and pulled on the ends as he turned his body so his side was facing me. "Fuck, Vi, this was never meant to happen. It was meant to be a little fun, but now…" He turned to face me. "I need… I…shit!"

"Spit it out, Axel." My voice was confident, but my insides were quaking because this was what I'd wanted to hear the day he drove me to the airport.

"I need to be with you."

My heart thumped in my chest, my pulse racing as fast as a racehorse on a track. "It won't work," I told him, but even I didn't believe myself. However much I tried to say it couldn't happen, I couldn't deny the feelings flowing through me when I sat and watched his photo at night with Colonel Fourpaws.

"Go on a date with me," he announced, stepping forward but stopping before touching me. "Let me do this right and take you out."

I bit down on my bottom lip. "I don't know…"

"One date. If you don't want to see me again, I'll obey your command."

I raised a brow. "You will, will you?"

He tried to keep a straight face, but he failed when I grinned at him. "I will. Anything you say goes."

"Anything?" I pushed off the counter. "Don't make promises you can't keep, Mr. Taylor." I placed my hand on his lapel and smoothed it out. "Pick me up at eight tomorrow with a box of cat treats, and you have yourself a date."

"Really?"

I walked toward the door. "Really, but you have to go." I tapped my empty wrist. "I'm on the clock."

I pulled the door open and waited for him to move toward me.

"Tomorrow then?"

"Tomorrow."

He leaned down, and I closed my eyes as he placed a kiss on my cheek, but he hovered longer as he breathed me in. I'd be a liar, liar, pants on fire if I said I wasn't doing the same.

I opened my eyes when he pulled back and stared at him as he walked out. He headed toward a shiny, black sports car parked outside, and as he opened the door, I shouted, "Don't you need to know where I live?"

"Nope." He turned to face me. "I'll find you."

It wasn't until he pulled away and was driving down the street that I realized he'd found me here.

What a freaking stalker!

Chapter 16

CONFESSION #10: I DROPPED MY
HAIRBRUSH DOWN THE TOILET... IS IT
OKAY TO USE AGAIN ORRRR?

Twisting to the left, I took a good look at myself. Hair slicked back into a high ponytail, my makeup on point and masking my black eye. A flowing, navy-blue jumpsuit covered my body and accentuated my curves.

"I don't scrub up too bad, huh, Colonel Fourpaws?" He sat on the end of the bed, watching me with keen eyes and probably wondering what all this extra effort I put into my appearance was all about.

Butterflies took flight in my stomach as I faced the mirror again. I should have told Axel to go and swivel, but instead, I'd caved. *Not tonight though.* I wanted to know what had been going on. Or was that pushing it too much? It was meant to be a little fun, nothing serious, yet, in my mind, I was practically married to the guy.

Good old feelings, huh.

Knocking echoed throughout my apartment and my stomach dipped. Colonel Fourpaws—ever the protector—jumped off the bed, strolled into the living room, leaped onto the arm of the sofa, and sat like a sentinel.

Taking a deep breath, I told myself it was only Axel and slipped my feet into my strappy heels and headed toward the door. I pulled on the handle and opened it. "Hey." My gaze ran the length of him, taking in his suit pants and shirt, especially the V where he'd left the first couple of buttons undone. I swallowed against the lump in my throat when he stayed silent.

His gaze tracked me, but he finally met my eyes, his dark-blue orbs flaring with unbridled passion. "Hey," he replied finally, his voice deep and husky.

We both stood there, taking each other in, a thousand things said with only our eyes. It was kind of awkward. I wasn't a person who did well with silence, so I always felt the need to fill the space with stupid words that escaped without any control.

"Want to meet my pussy?" *Annnd that's exactly what I meant.* I slapped my palm on my forehead, laughing awkwardly. "I mean, my cat. Do you want to meet my cat?"

His lips lifted into a smirk as he handed me a small packet. I looked down at them and had to contain the huge grin that wanted to take over my face. He'd remembered the cat treats.

I moved to the side, but I didn't move enough for him to come inside. Nope. No. Because if he stepped inside this apartment, I knew I wouldn't be able to control myself.

"Colonel Fourpaws, meet Axel. Axel," I waved my arm toward the cat. "Meet my new cat, Colonel Fourpaws."

He didn't say anything and scrunched his face up. I swung my gaze back to Axel and raised a brow. "Well... say hi, then."

He huffed. "I'm not talking to a cat."

"If I remember rightly, you're very vocal when it comes to pussies." I bit down on my bottom lip as I silently screamed to shut the hell up!

He took a step toward me, his eyes flashing with promises, and suddenly I was panicking, becoming the fourteen-year-old girl about to have her first kiss.

Abort! Abort!

"Shall we get going?" I asked and grabbed my purse.

I rushed out the door and practically knocked him over. It didn't deter me from hurrying out of the confined space and slamming the door behind me. I power walked down the hallway and the stairs, making it out into the warm LA air. I halted on the sidewalk and took a breath. How did he make my body and brain go completely haywire when he was close to me?

Axel's hand grazed my lower back, and I jumped, my hand flying to my chest. "Stop freaking out. It's only me."

"Only you," I snorted, glancing up at him. "You have no idea the effect you have on people."

He dipped his head down and whispered, "Neither do you," and stood to his full height, his eyes piercing mine. "You're beautiful, as always."

I nodded, not knowing what to say. For the last six weeks all I'd done was sit and stare at his picture, feeling like the time we had together was a dream. But now he was here, in the flesh, taking me on a date. *A date.*

"You hungry?" he asked, intensifying the force in his palm on my back to silently tell me to walk.

"Starved."

"Great." He stepped toward the same sports car he

was driving yesterday and opened up the door. "I know a great place."

"Sure," I replied and slipped into the passenger seat.

I was an awkward mess, and he was gonna know how much of a freak I was. *He already knows,* a voice said in the back of my mind. I told the voice to shut the hell up as I stuffed a metaphorical banana in her mouth.

He turned the engine on, and the air conditioner blasted me in the face. His hands gripped the steering wheel as he maneuvered the car onto the road, and I couldn't stop staring at how he moved without a second thought. Why did he have to be so freaking hot? Couldn't he look like an ogre or something? It would make this whole situation so much easier.

"Why?" I blurted out after five minutes of silence.

He side-eyed me, raising a brow. "Why, what?"

"Why are you doing this?"

"Taking you out on a date?"

"Yeah, duh."

He chuckled. "Because I want to."

He pulled up outside a seafood restaurant, bringing the car to a halt without any effort. I swallowed as he slid out and kept my focus on him as he walked around to my door and opened it.

"I don't get it."

We strolled toward the double glass doors, Axel's hand automatically resting at the bottom of my back. He didn't answer me as he pulled the doors open and moved toward a woman standing behind a wooden stand. She smiled wide at him and instructed him to follow her. Axel extended his hand to me, and I took it without a second thought, following them to a table toward the back.

"Can I get you anything to drink?" she asked when we're sitting down.

"I'll take a water. Vi?"

"Glass of white wine, please."

"Any particular kind?" she questioned.

I glanced around at all the tables full of people smiling and having fun. "Erm...any will do," I told her, the nerves taking me over full force as I peeked back at Axel.

I'd had sex with this man, worked for him, gone out with him. But this? A proper date? It was making me a nervous wreck. I wished he would have taken me for a burger. I was so out of my element, and I knew for a fact it was showing.

"Because I can't stop thinking about you," Axel announced when the waitress had left.

"Huh?"

He clasped my hand on the table, leaning forward. "Because not having you around is lonely. Because all I can see when I close my eyes is your smiling face. I miss your voice, I miss your klutziness, I miss *you*." His lips spread into a genuine smile. "That's why I'm here in LA —taking you out."

"I thought you were here for work?" I asked, not wanting to address everything he'd said. My brain was on overload, a red flashing warning screaming inside, telling me I was going to explode any second.

He shook his head, keeping my hand encased in his. "I could've done what I needed to on a video call, but I wanted to see you."

I laughed. "And I wasn't there."

The waitress placed our drinks on the table, stopping

our conversation briefly, and then he said, "I really didn't know what happened, Vi. I swear."

"Yeah, well…" I averted my attention. "I think she was planning to do it before I even landed. She asked to see me when she called before Christmas."

"If I could fire her and get someone else to run—"

"No," I interrupted. "I don't want anything to do with her being fired. I want to start over. Fresh start and all that."

"Does that include us?" he asked, his eyes filled with hope. I wanted to tell him yes, but something was guarding my heart right now, so I stayed silent.

Why was adulting so hard?

———

"We shouldn't be doing this," I moaned as Axel trailed kisses up my neck, walking me backward down the hallway to my apartment door.

After the best seafood I'd ever tasted, and a bottle of wine to myself, I was feeling a little merry. Not enough to not know what was going on, but enough to let my worries evaporate into thin air.

"Hmmm."

"Axel." My eyes rolled into the back of my head as he sucked the skin on my neck and pushed me against the wall. His hips thrust, and I felt the hardness of his dick pressing against my stomach. My hand had a mind of its own as it reached down and stroked him over his pants.

"God, Vi." He threw his head back.

My lips spread into a smirk at the reaction I got, and it was right at that moment that I knew I'd never felt this same way about anyone else. He brought out a side in me that no one else ever had. Not only that, but he made me feel like I was the most beautiful person in a room full of people.

"Let me inside," he groaned, bringing his face close to mine.

"Is that a euphemism? You want inside my apartment, orrrr, inside my vagina?"

He dropped his lips to mine, pushed his tongue inside, and twirled it with mine. My hands gripped his shoulders, jerking him as close as I could.

"Both," he murmured when he pulled away. He wrapped his arms around my waist and picked me up. My legs automatically locked around his hips, and I thrust against him, causing us both to moan.

"Mine is the next door down," I told him—as if he didn't already know—and dipped my head, trailing kisses down his neck as he moved us off the wall and paced forward.

"Keys," he demanded.

I handed him my purse, silently telling him they were in there as I continued my ministrations. After several minutes, he managed to open my door and maneuver us inside. I continued thrusting, and he growled, slamming the door behind us.

"Fuck, I need you so bad right now."

I lifted my head, planted a kiss on his lips, and pushed my fingers through his hair. "I'm here, take me."

"Fuck me, those words…say them again."

I lowered my voice. "Take me, Axel. Fuck me harder than you ever have."

He pushed me up against the door, let me down, and then yanked the front zip on my jumpsuit. He jerked it off me, and I swayed to the side at his eagerness, surprised but loving it all at the same time.

This was hot. He was hot. God, why was I feeling so hot right now?

He crouched down, took my heels off, stood, and picked me up again. The room spun as he twirled us around, only it didn't stop rotating when he sat down on the sofa. His long fingers tugged my bra straps down, and I placed my hand on the top of his head, trying to center myself.

"Axel?"

"I know, baby. I'll make you feel—"

"No—"

"No?" he asked, pulling back and staring at me like I had two heads.

My hand covered my mouth as I swayed to the side. "I'm gonna be sick." My stomach churned, my mouth watering as he drew back.

"What?"

"I'm gonna throw up!"

I tried to get off him, but the room spun even more and made it even worse. He grabbed for me and lifted us off the sofa as he asked, "Bathroom?"

"That door." My muscles moved slowly, but I managed to point to the door.

He pushed it open and placed me on the floor just in time for me to throw up all that amazing seafood.

Well, that went well…not.

Chapter 17

CONFESSION #88: I SLIPPED IN THE
SHOWER AND TRIED TO GRAB WATER...
BECAUSE THAT WILL SAVE ME.

I stared out the window as we landed at JFK, gripping the piece of paper Axel left for me the morning after the epic disaster that was our date.

When I woke up in my underwear and in bed without him there, I was sure I'd scared him away with my epic throw-up session. But when I walked into the living room and saw his scrawl on an envelope, I didn't know what to think.

I looked down, opening the note up and reading it for literally the thousandth time.

Vi,
Before your brain starts working overtime, I had to go back to New York for an emergency meeting, but I wish I was still there with you.
Seeing you again made up my mind.
I can't live without you, Vi. <—That wasn't some corny line. I MEAN it.
Even if you have to stay in LA, we can make this work.

*I know we can because I have a feeling you feel the
same way.*

*I'm crazy about you, have been since you showed up in
my office and ripped your skirt. (Loved those panties,
by the way.)*

*Just know I want to be with you…only you. My plan
went to shit yesterday when I saw you. I was meant to
be romantic and hold myself back, but I never can
where you're concerned.*

*Soooo… Without sounding like a ten-year-old on the
playground, will you be my girlfriend?*

PS. Love where you have my picture. ;)

Axel.

My lips spread into the widest smile because as
corny as it sounded, I knew he meant every word. When
I realized he knew where I kept the picture of us, I
started to panic. But then I got to thinking, what did it
matter? However much I liked to try and deny it, I'd
fallen head over heels for him, too, and now I needed to
do something about it.

The airplane came to a stop, and everyone started to
stand, readying themselves to disembark the plane and
enter the terminal. Nerves flowed through me at break-
neck speed as I stepped off the plane and onto New York
soil. I didn't know what was making me more anxious:
the meeting with the publishing company or pulling my
plan off for Axel.

I knew what I wanted to do as soon as I read his
letter, but I'd been radio silent since. No reason not to
make him wait, right?

Grabbing my carry-on, deja vu assailed me as I moved through the airport, only this time Jeeves wasn't there to greet me. Instead, I took a taxi to the hotel the publishing company had arranged for me. One thing I hadn't missed about New York was the crazy taxi drivers. They were their own special breed here.

After I'd checked in and gone up to my room, I threw my case on the bed, yanked my cell out, and FaceTimed JJ. It rang and rang, and when I was about to end it, he answered, his face coming into view but waaay too close.

I chuckled. "Pull it away a little, JJ."

He did, and I could tell he was extending his arm as far as he could. "Violet," he greeted.

"Hey, JJ. Just checking in. How's Colonel Fourpaws?"

"He ate a packet of food and two treats. He's slept for three hours and bathed himself." He spun the screen around, showing me where the cat was sitting on his lap. "He's asleep again." He turned it back to face him. "Did you know cats sleep between sixteen and twenty hours a day?"

"I didn't," I said, a small smile on my face. "Is he behaving himself?"

"Yes," he answered, his lips lifting up into a ghost of a smile. "I used to have a cat. She was black and loved cuddles. Colonel Fourpaws loves cuddles, too."

"He does."

"You look stressed," JJ noted, his brows scrunching.

"I'm just nervous." I swiped my hand over my forehead. "What if they don't like any of them? What if this is a waste of time?"

I didn't expect JJ to answer, so when he said, "You'll

get the job. My tummy says so," I couldn't help but feel relieved.

"Thanks, JJ."

"For what?"

"Looking after Colonel Fourpaws and being my friend."

"I like friends. I have two. You and my dad."

I smiled, but it was a sad kind of smile. If only more people would take the time to get to know him. They'd be surprised at how much love he had to give.

I lifted my head and noticed the time on the clock. "Crap. I gotta go! I'll call you later!"

"Okay, bye." The screen went black, and I chuckled at his abrupt farewell.

———

I glanced up at the building—you guessed it: glass and metal. This city was obsessed with them, and I still didn't get the appeal.

My hand slipped on the handle of my leather bag containing some of my drawings. The nerves were rife. I thought even my nerves were nervous. Several people walked out the doors, busy on their cells or talking to people while I stood in the middle of the sidewalk staring up at the building with the giant letters "FGT" displayed above the doors. This meeting could change my life. It could change everything…

Or nothing.

Taking a deep breath, I steeled myself and put one foot in front of the other. I strolled inside and was amazed by the foyer. There were posters everywhere of the covers of bestselling books, docks where laptops sat for people to use all over the place, and little alcoves where people were curled up reading.

I couldn't work out where the front desk was, so when someone stepped past me with a headset on, I moved into his line of sight.

"Hi, do you know where the front desk is?"

He lifted his arm and pointed to the left. "Over there."

I turned to see where he was pointing, saying, "Thanks," as I turned back around, but he was already gone. "Well, okay then."

I ambled over to the desk, waited for the woman on a call to finish, and stepped forward. "Hi, my name is Violet Scott, I have a meeting with—"

"Larry De'lanto."

"I... I think so," I replied, my voice seeming to have left my body. Crap, I'd never felt like this before.

"Take a seat." She signaled to a couple of white, leather sofas. "He'll be down to collect you when he's ready."

"Right, okay."

She smiled, and I headed over to the sofas. Sitting down on the edge of one, I held my leather bag to my chest and watched as everyone came in and out of the doors. There was a group of people gathered to one side, all staring at a tablet and conversing. The atmosphere was easy, the people seeming friendly with looks of pleasure on their faces. These people loved what they did. The sight was strange to see, but I found myself wanting to appear the same way.

"Miss Scott?"

My head snapped up at the deep voice, and I stood, teetering on the heels I was wearing. "That's me." I righted myself, stepped forward, and extended my hand slowly, trying to be more aware of my surroundings.

He clasped my hand. "Nice to meet you, I'm Larry." His dark-brown hair was graying at the temples, wrinkles showing around his eyes when he smiled, but his face was kind.

"Violet," I replied.

He extended his arm. "Shall we?"

"Sure."

I followed him up a staircase in the middle of the foyer, down a hallway filled with more posters of best-selling books, and into a conference room where three other people were waiting.

"This is Shelly, Lawrence, and Tanya."

"Nice to meet you." I shook their hands in turn, cringing at the fact they could probably feel the sweat on mine. Ack.

Sitting down opposite them all, I waited while Larry explained to me what they did, the kind of books they were publishing at the moment, and how the market was always changing.

"We recently branched out into children's books and are wanting to go into the graphic novel market." He folded his hands on top of the big conference table. "That's where you come in. One of our authors forwarded your drawings."

"Yes." I cleared my throat. "My cousin was doing some graphic design work for her and showed her them."

Tanya sat up straighter. "Is this something you like to do? Draw?"

"I…" I paused. "I've never felt more at home than when I have a pen in my hand, creating something. I'm passionate about all different styles." I unzipped my leather bag and pulled some of my drawings out. "I can do soft and cuddly, but also horror, and anything in between."

Pushing them across the table, I waited with bated breath as they all took their turn to look at them. I couldn't tell what any of them were thinking, not one flicker of any emotion in their eyes or on their faces. Crap. They didn't like them—

"And you're based in LA?" Lawrence asked.

"I am, but relocating wouldn't be a problem. I don't have ties there." My heart panged when I thought of JJ, but I pushed that to the side.

"We do like to have our illustrators in house." He tilted his head to the side. "Makes things easier with the line of work we're in."

"Of course." I smiled brightly—too brightly, I probably looked like the freaking Joker.

They all started to murmur between themselves, the hand of the clock ticking away and shouting at me with every second that went by. Larry passed me my drawings and stood. I took it as my cue to do the same, so I balanced my bag against my stomach and slipped the drawings back inside while simultaneously standing.

Was this all they wanted? Basically to see my face?

"Thanks for coming in today. We'll be in touch."

I stepped toward the door but couldn't stop myself from blurting out, "Is that a 'we'll be in touch but not really' kind of be in touch? Or a 'we'll *actually* be in touch' kind of in touch?"

Lawrence chuckled, his gaze meeting mine as he stood too. "It's a, 'we'll be in touch' kind of in touch."

"Oh, right. Awesome… Well, thanks for seeing me."

I stepped out of the room with Larry behind me, and we both walked back down the stairs and to the main foyer.

Larry held his hand out. "It was nice to meet you."

"You too." I placed mine in his.

He let go, gave me one last nod, and twirled around. I stared at him as he walked back up the stairs, wondering if maybe he'd turn around any second and hand me a job. *Yeah, right.*

I rotated on the spot in a circle, wishing like hell I *did* get this job because I felt in my bones this was meant to be.

———

I slipped my cell into my purse with *the* biggest grin on my face as I stepped out of the elevator and glanced back at Al. "Thanks, Al."

"You're welcome, Miss Scott."

I stared at the doors as they closed and then sauntered inside Axel's penthouse suite. My gaze tracked everything, taking it all in and feeling like I just entered my own home. Whether it was his office, his home, or him, he just felt like home, like I was meant to be right there with him.

Tentatively, I stepped forward, knowing I was here alone, but it was perfect for my plan. My lips lifted into a smirk as I walked toward his bedroom. I'd spent seven days planning this, and I knew he definitely wouldn't see it coming.

I removed my jacket, set it down on the chair in the corner of the room, and placed my bag next to it. I spun around, observing the huge bed Axel slept in, the gray bedding, and the bedside tables on either side. Sitting down on the edge of the bed, I pulled in a deep breath, wondering if this was the best way to do this.

Who was I kidding? Of course it was!

I stood and started to undress until I was left in only the black lace bra and panties, complete with suspenders and stockings. I know, I know, I'd gone all out. But you could only accept a girlfriend proposal once, right?

I left my heels on and sat on the edge of the bed and waited...and waited. I became restless and stood, alternating between pacing and sitting with my legs crossed. A half hour ticked by, and I knew he'd be here any second.

A door opened in the main room, and my eyes widened. I got into position, lying on my side, one leg over the other, and propping my head on my hand, listening as the footsteps stopped outside the bedroom door. My heart beat wildly in my chest as someone murmured, and then the door handle moved, and the door opened and revealed...*Marcus—Axel's dad*.

His wide-eyed gaze met mine and I scrambled off the bed, trying to search for something to cover myself. I grabbed onto the end of the bedding and yanked, expecting it to come free, but it didn't because it was tucked under the mattress.

Why did the housekeepers make beds like this? It was a stupid, stupid system!

"Dad?" Axel called, his footsteps nearing. "Did you find it?"

Marcus stepped back, his mouth opening and closing, but no sound was coming out as a shadow fell over him.

"Dad?"

Axel moved closer, and his face came into view, but his attention was focused solely on Marcus as I continued to try and pull the stupid bedding off to give me some dignity. *Goddamn, shit!*

His gaze met mine finally, widening as it tracked over my near-naked body, a grin working its way over his lips. "Vi?"

I straightened and used my hands to try and cover some skin, yet it was no use because I had two boobs and one vagina but only two hands.

His dad stepped to the side, spun around, and muttered, "I…erm… I… I'm gonna go."

Axel chuckled, not moving his attention from me as he said, "I'll call you later, Dad."

His dad marched away, and a door slammed somewhere, signaling he'd left.

The air stilled as Axel stepped forward. "What are you doing, Vi?"

"Surprise?" I croaked, moving my arms out beside me. "I'm back."

"You're back?" he asked, stalking toward me.

I nodded. "I got your letter, and I accept."

"You accept?" He raised a brow as he came to a stop a few inches away, not one part of his body touching mine.

"Your girlfriend proposal: I accept."

He chuckled, shaking his head, his eyes lighting up. And then he frowned. "I know it'll be hard with you in LA—"

"I won't be in LA," I told him, closing the distance between us. "I just got offered a job here in New York."

He raised his hands, cupping either side of my face. "You did?"

"Mmm-hmm, I'm the newest employee of FGT Publishing. They want me to illustrate their books."

I grinned when I thought about the call I had while I was riding the elevator. I'd started the day with a job in a pet store, and I was ending it with my dream career about to get started *and* an Adonis for a boyfriend. Check me out!

"No way."

"Yes way."

He smiled wide, a genuine smile that said so much more than any of his words ever could. "I knew you'd make it back here."

"Back where?" I asked, lifting up on my tiptoes as he tilted his head down.

"Back in my arms."

I laughed at his corniness, placed my lips against his, and got caught up in all that was Axel. His hands feathered over the soft skin covering my ribs, and then he suddenly gripped harder, and threw me on the bed. This time there'd be no throwing up like the "disaster date" as I dubbed it.

Only orgasms.

Lots and lots of orgasms.

Thank You!

Thank you so much for reading this book! If you loved it as much as I did writing it, then please consider leaving a review.

Be In The Know

If you're nosey like me and want exclusive snippets and sneak peaks, you'll find them in my newsletter!

BE NOSEY, CLICK HERE

Also by Abigail Davies

MAC Security Series

Book 1: Fractured Lies

Book 2: Exposed

Book 2.5: Flying Free (Standalone Spin-off)

Book 3: The Distance Between Us

Book 4: ReBoot

Book 5: Catching Teardrops

Six Book Boxset

Confessions Series

Book 1: Confessions Of A Klutz

Book 2: Confessions Of A Chatterbox

Book 3: Confessions Of A Fratgirl

Fallen Duet

Book 1: Free Fall

Book 2: Down Fall

Broken Tracks Series,
co-authored with Danielle Dickson

Book 1: Etching Our Way

Book 2: Fighting Our Way

Destroyed Series,
co-authored with L. Grubb

Destroying the Game

Destroying the Soul

About the Author

Abigail Davies grew up with a passion for words, story-telling, maths, and anything pink. Dreaming up characters—quite literally—and talking to them out loud is a daily occurrence for her. She finds it fascinating how a whole world can be built with words alone, and how everyone reads and interprets a story differently. Now following her dreams of writing, Abigail has found the passion that she always knew was there. When she's not writing: she's a mother to two daughters who she encourages to use their imagination as she believes that it's a magical thing, or getting lost in a good book. If she's doing neither of those things, you can be sure she's surfing the web buying new makeup, clothes, or binge watching another show as she becomes one with her sofa.

Connect with Abigail

Reader group—Abi's Aces
Newsletter
www.abigaildaviesauthor.com

facebook.com/abigaildaviesauthor

twitter.com/abigailadavies

instagram.com/abigaildaviesauthor

goodreads.com/abigaildavies

bookbub.com/authors/abigail-davies

amazon.com/author/abigaildavies

pinterest.com/abigaildaviesauthor

Made in the USA
Columbia, SC
23 November 2021

49660155R00133